I0747741

A Light in the Window

Also by Dan Lutts:

Charm Wars

A Light in the Window

A *CHARM WARS* FANTASY NOVEL
BOOK 2

Dan Lutts

Castine Press

Penobscot, Maine

Copyright © 2022 by Dan Lutts.

All rights reserved. No part of this publication may be reproduced, distributed or transmitted in any form or by any means, including photocopying, recording, or other electronic or mechanical methods, without the prior written permission of the publisher, except in the case of brief quotations embodied in critical reviews and certain other noncommercial uses permitted by copyright law. For permission requests, write to the publisher, addressed "Attention: Permissions Coordinator," at the address below.

Dan Lutts / Castine Press

P.O. Box 26

Penobscot, Maine 04476

DanLutts.com

Book Layout ©2017 BookDesignTemplates.com

A Light in the Window / Dan Lutts —1st ed.

ISBN 978-1-7353592-5-0

Contents

To my parents, Jean and Herb,
who always supported me in my writing

*I'll lead my own life—even if it means being denounced
by my family*

— Alyse Dejune

I'll bring Alyse back, no matter what, and make Lord Deuth proud he took me on as his apprentice mage.

— Rill Larkin

Map of Caldon

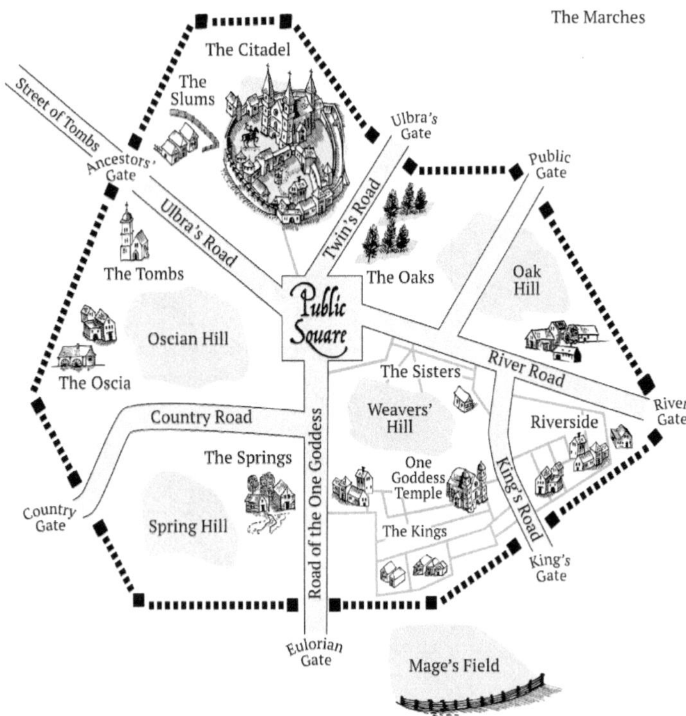

The Marches
The Citadel
The Slums
Street of Tombs
Ancestors' Gate
Ulbra's Gate
Public Gate
Ulbra's Road
Twin's Road
The Tombs
The Oaks
Oak Hill
Public Square
Oscian Hill
River Road
The Sisters
The Oscia
Weavers' Hill
Riverside
River Gate
Country Road
One Goddess Temple
King's Road
The Springs
Road of the One Goddess
The Kings
Country Gate
Spring Hill
King's Gate
Eulorian Gate
Mage's Field

N

Charm World
Forbidden Lands
Mittan
Rocky Strait
The Marches
Fraedia
Caldon
Inland Sea
Caldonia
Ostica
Annatol
Anglia
Gaetan
Cyrene
Gaetania
N

Flight

TOWARD EVENING, ALYSE DEJUNE and her cousin, Kate Dejune, rode along the dirt road into a sleepy town nestled at the edge of a forest and stopped by an inn to water their horses at a trough while townspeople meandered along the sidewalks and street. The anxious throbbing of Alyse's heart sounded like rapid drumbeats in her ears. Caldon was only a half day's journey behind them, which allowed plenty of time for news of their flight from the city to reach here. Then she pressed her lips together in a grimace. She and Kate had been traveling at a medium canter to not tire their horses. Few people on horseback had passed them, and the ones who had, hadn't even given them a glance.

An icy stab of fear shot down Alyse's spine when she heard the faint but rapid sound of hoofbeats behind them. Horses running at full gallop. She swapped panicked looks with Kate. "They've come after us!"

Alyse glanced wildly around for some place to hide, just as someone in the inn across from them put candles on the windowsills. "We'll go in there!"

She and Kate scrambled down from their saddles. But they had reacted too late as a woman and two men on horseback galloped into town. The cousins put their hands on the hilts of their swords, readying themselves for battle.

"Here they come again," a woman's irritated voice said from somewhere behind them.

"I sure wish they'd go to some other town," a man responded. "I'm gettin' sure tired of 'em comin' here to raise the dickens."

Other townspeople muttered their agreement.

The three drew rein by the tavern, scooted off their horses, and disappeared inside.

Alyse's anxiety gushed out of her body like a rapidly flowing river, and she swapped relieved looks with Kate. She uttered a shaky laugh. "I'd call that overreacting."

Kate sent her a tight smile. "Same here."

Alyse glanced up and down the street. Now that the newcomers had disappeared, everyone had returned to their own business. Some walked along the sidewalks while others went into the inn as oil lamps were lit in its two unshuttered front windows, emitting warm, welcoming glows. The inn's lanterns must have been a signal to the other townspeople because, one by one, dancing yellowish flames from candles and oil lamps in the windows of the shops, taverns, and homes lining both sides of the road began appearing.

Alyse and Kate traded relieved looks.

"If anyone's chasing after us," Alyse said, "they're still behind us."

"Thank Goddess for that."

Alyse and Kate brushed road dust off their nondescript commoners' rough woolen pants and vests and white linen shirts, then stretched their aching muscles. Kate watered their mares and refilled their canteens from a small circular fountain in the town.

Alyse glanced up the road that disappeared into the gloomy forest beyond the town. The sight of the woods sent dread slinking across her shoulders. She had never spent the night outside of Caldon before, except for the times she had stayed at her family's villa in the country. And the prospect of sleeping tonight in the forest, surrounded by trees and wild animals and Goddess knew what else, gave her the chills. "I wish we could spend the night here."

Kate handed Alyse a canteen heavy with water. "We can't. We've barely put a half-day's distance between us and Caldon—"

Alyse pulled out her canteen stopper and swallowed a mouthful of cool water. "Mora told us she'd delay telling my parents we'd run away. But I bet she went right home and told Grandmother Maude. I can just picture the glee on her face as she's doing it."

Kate nodded in agreement.

"Then Grandmother will expel me from the family, and Mora can marry Troy Estati instead of me." Alyse paused, then added heartfelt words. "And she's welcome to him."

Kate wrapped her canteen's strap around her saddle pommel. "Even if Mora kept her word, and I'm sure she didn't, she knows we left by the Public Gate. That's the road to The Marches. It leads to your uncle's legionary camp there."

"We have to reach Uncle Leoc before they catch up to us." Alyse pushed the wood stopper into the canteen's mouth. "He'll protect us."

"You hope."

"He gave me his word."

"He might be the Commander of the Eastern Legions, but he's also subject to the Magesterium. If they order him to hand you over, he will."

Alyse tightened her saddle's cinch, suddenly eager to set off again. "He won't. Unless he crosses the border into Caldonian territory, the Magesterium can only suggest, not command. Besides, the Magesterium won't get involved because this dispute doesn't involve the state. It's between two families."

"Which happen to be among the most powerful in Caldon." Kate brushed back strands of black hair from her forehead. "It's the matriarchs who pull the strings in the Magesterium. If your Grandmother Maude and Ariella Estati—"

"The Dejune and Estati matriarchs won't involve the Magesterium. And Uncle Leoc won't hand me over to my grandmother. He'll smooth things over."

"I don't think so," Kate muttered.

"Besides you," Alyse said, "Uncle Leoc is the only person in the whole world I trust. He'll keep his promise."

"He's defeated Mittan, and he'll want to celebrate his victory by holding a magnificent triumph on his return to Caldon when his term of service ends.

If he succeeds in defeating any of the other countries, he'll want to have an even greater celebration. He'll be allowed to bring some of his legions back as well to take part in his triumph. And I bet your enemy First and Lesser Families will do everything they can to prevent him from having his victory celebration. Your uncle would be furious if he was denied his triumph. Goddess knows what would happen then. He might even want to overthrow the state."

A coldness gripped Alyse while her mind rebelled against Kate's accusation. "He would *never* do that."

Kate shrugged. "It's too late now for second thoughts. We have to see this through and hope your uncle keeps his word."

"He will."

Kate eyed the forest, creases of apprehension working their way into her face. Alyse was relieved to see that her cousin was just as frightened of the forest as she was.

"Let's get going." Kate mounted her gray mare. "We have lots of distance to cover."

Alyse swung into her saddle, then pointed her mare's head toward the forest. She and Kate started off at a walk.

A couple of passersby eyed them curiously, but one elderly man stepped into the street, blocking their path. "You girls headin' into the forest?"

"That's our business," Alyse said.

"That's Malagnar Forest yonder. There's brigands holed up in there. Wise travelers don't pass through Malagnar Forest except in groups. And they avoid it at night." The man pointed to the inn. "I'd stay there tonight if I was you."

"We'll keep that in mind," Alyse said.

With a shrug, the man stepped aside. "Don't say I didn't warn ya."

Moving past him, Alyse urged her bay mare into a trot. Kate kept pace beside her.

"Travel fast," the man shouted after them. "And don't stop for nothin'."

As soon as Alyse entered the forest, tall pines and trees bristling with leaves loomed up on either side of her, creating a partial canopy that threw the road into shadow. She'd never been this far east before, and she'd never heard of Malagnar Forest. The forest's name sounded ominous. Alyse recalled the man's warning and her heart tightened with dread as she suppressed a shudder.

Alyse didn't go too far along the dirt road, riding side by side with Kate, before Kate reined in her horse. "We're breaking for food."

Alyse peered uneasily at the darkening woods. "I thought we were riding straight through."

"We are," Kate responded. "But we should eat first and give the horses more of a breather. We won't get any more food or rest until we reach the other side of the forest. And Goddess knows when that'll be."

Dismounting, Alyse and Kate led their mares behind a clump of bushes a short way off the road and tied the reins to branches, unfastened feedbags from their saddles, and fed the horses. Afterward, they settled down on a fallen tree trunk with their own travelers' fare—a loaf of crusty bread, a large hunk of cheese, and a leather wine pouch.

They ate in silence as the sun began its slow descent behind the forest canopy. Hoots came from somewhere nearby, sending shivers down Alyse's spine. She traded nervous looks with Kate. Then, as if on cue, they both uttered nervous laughter.

"We're city girls through and through," Alyse said.

Kate bobbed her head in agreement. "Take some poor villager and put her in the city, and she'd be just as frightened."

"Rill told me once that he goes into the woods hunting with Jedd—" Alyse stopped abruptly as memories of her last encounter with Rill Larkin flooded her mind. Or, rather, memories of what he'd done to Dayson Florens, the wine-shop owner she'd treated at the One Goddess Temple.

Rill had beaten up the old man to force him to sign over the larger share of his business to the Estatis for not repaying money he'd borrowed from them. Rill's lust for becoming a mage had made him into an Estati thug.

Alyse exchanged a quick glance with Kate, who appeared just as troubled by the dark thoughts Rill's name had conjured up.

"At least Jedd had the good sense to walk away from it all," Kate said.

Alyse couldn't hide the sadness in her voice. "And it's too bad Rill didn't walk away too. Deep down, he's a good person. But the Estatis have led him astray to get back at his mother."

Kate took a sip of watered red wine from the pouch. "I still can't believe it. Kendra Larkin is actually Deuth Estati's older sister, who renounced her family and married Rill's father, a commoner and a blacksmith. Livia Estati is really Rill's half sister. And her brother, Troy, is actually her cousin. And Rill's too. Phew! That's enough to confuse anyone. Can you blame Rill—"

Leaves rustled off to their right. Kate jumped to her feet, half drawing her sword. Alyse gripped the handle of her dagger and held her breath, listening for more sounds and peering at the dark, dense foliage. The mares snorted and pawed the leaf-covered ground. An animal's high-pitched scream erupted from deeper in the forest. The horses snorted again and jerked at their reins, making the leaf-covered branches bend.

Alyse and Kate swapped fearful looks.

"What was that?" Alyse asked in a tense whisper.

"An invitation to be off," Kate replied.

Alyse and Kate hastily unfastened their mares' reins from the branches, led them back onto the road, and continued on their way at a trot. Soon sunset turned into twilight and eventually into darkness. To Alyse's relief, the partial canopy of branches and leaves allowed the full moon's pale light to shine through, revealing the contours of the road as a barely visible carpet running between thick walls of blackness.

Even though they were halfway through First Fruits, the hottest season of the year, the air grew chilly. Alyse took her light woolen cloak from her saddlebag and wrapped it around herself. After a while, she lost all sense of time and distance as her body moved in rhythm to her mare's gait. The sounds of the horses' hooves on the hard-packed dirt weren't loud enough to deaden the terrifying barks, screeches, screams, and howls that continuously erupted in the woods. Fear clutched at Alyse each time she heard them.

To Alyse, it seemed as if the journey through the gloomy, sinister forest was taking forever. She was an occasional rider, not a frequent one. And she'd been in the saddle for so long that the muscles in her buttocks, thighs, and legs sent out sharp pains in time to the drumming of her horse's iron-shod hooves against the road.

"Let's stop for just a short time," Alyse said. "I can't stay in the saddle much longer."

"All right," Kate responded, hesitancy in her voice.

Alyse stood in her stirrups and began to move her right foot over her mare's rear—and froze. "Brigands!" she yelled. She swung her foot back into the stirrup and drew her sword.

Dark figures charged into the road from both sides of the forest.

"Get 'em!" a rough voice shouted.

A hand closed on Alyse's leg. Whipping out her dagger, Alyse stabbed the hand. The attacker yelped in pain and let go. Then murky figures brandishing swords and clubs surged around her mare, trying to wrest Alyse out of the saddle. Alyse slashed at them wildly. But as soon as one attacker fell away, two more seemed to come at her. Frantically, Alyse tried to kick the horse into a gallop but more brigands barred the way. The mare reared, almost unseating Alyse.

All of a sudden Kate appeared, swinging her sword at the attackers and opening a path for the mare. "Ride!"

Alyse dug her heals into the mare's flanks, and the horse exploded into a gallop.

A dark form lunged at Alyse as the mare sped by. Alyse cut at the brigand with her dagger, slicing through flesh and bone. The attacker screamed and stumbled back.

And then Alyse broke free of the brigands. Her first thought was for Kate.

Galloping hoofbeats sounded behind her.

"Keep going!" Kate cried.

Alyse rode furiously, with Kate chasing after her. Alyse's heart beat fiercely against her rib cage, striving to ignore the desperate pounding of her bay's hooves against the ground. In her mind, she felt the brigand's hand on her leg. A shudder swept through her body. *If he'd unhorsed me—* She kicked the thought from her mind. He hadn't.

Kate drew up beside her, and they rode together. After a while, Kate slowed down to a trot, and Alyse matched the pace. Finally, Alyse pulled in on her reins. Kate did too.

"Are you all right?" Alyse asked as she strove to get her breathing under control.

"Just a few nicks," Kate said. "I think we surprised them with our spirited defense."

"You did. Not me." Alyse raked her fingers through her reddish-brown hair. "I feel so vulnerable with just a dagger. I appreciate you teaching me how to use one. But when we get to Uncle Leoc's, I want you to teach me how to use a sword."

"You have your Kinesi magic."

"No!" The force of Alyse's outburst astonished even herself. She lowered her tone but kept it firm. "I won't use Kinesi magic. Or any other magic except Healing magic. Besides, I don't know how to summon the Kinesi power. I can only access it in times of stress. Sometimes not even then. And I don't know how to control it."

"If you learned how to summon and control it, you could use it whenever you wanted."

Alyse shook her head doggedly. "I won't use Kinesi magic."

"Kinesi magic can be better than a sword for some things. You've shown me that."

"I won't use it."

"Why?"

Alyse urged her mare closer to Kate's and spoke in a tone teeming with determination. "Magic is the root of all that's wrong in the world. First and Lesser Families raiding and killing one another for their charms and staffs. Conscripting fledging mages who don't receive patrons at The Bidding or who don't join the legions or the sea service. And this ages-long war with Gaetan. We started it because we wanted to recover the charms and staffs Toran the Usurper took with him when the Caldonians rebelled against him, and he fled the city to found Gaetan. Also—"

"All right. Point made. I'll teach you how to use a sword."

They broke free of the forest a little after dawn and stopped to eat a quick meal by the edge of the woods. Both girls' buttocks and thighs were sending them agonizing streaks of fire. Alyse applied healing hands to ease Kate's aching muscles.

"I wish you could use healing hands on yourself," Kate said as they waited for the healing magic to take effect.

"So do I," Alyse responded. "But a healer can't heal herself. Only others."

"We'll take more frequent breaks so you can stretch your legs," Kate told her.

"But our pursuers—"

"Probably haven't set out until this morning. We have a good lead on them. So I think we can afford to go a little slower."

Remounting, Alyse and Kate continued to ride.

As the sun climbed into the sky, they began passing farmers riding in wagons piled with produce or firewood, and fellow travelers on foot or on horseback. The road brought them through a combination of woodlands, hills, and open land dotted with small farms, a few large prosperous ones, and an occasional inn. Every so often a crossroads split off from the main road, but Alyse and Kate continued east. Once, Alyse spotted a young teenage girl fishing by the stream using a rod made from a stick and envied her carefree attitude.

Around midmorning, they passed through a village. By this time, both girls, who hadn't slept since the night before they left Caldon, were dozing in their saddles.

In the early afternoon, they entered a prosperous-looking town where they stopped to buy a flask of weak beer, a couple of cold meat pies for themselves, and grain for the horses. A short distance out of town they spotted a stand of trees and shrubs on a knoll that provided good concealment.

"I think it's time we got some sleep," Kate said.

Alyse heaved a relieved sigh. "At last!"

As Alyse swung down from the saddle, she stifled a groan and hobbled around to ease her aching muscles. Meanwhile, Kate unsaddled and fed the horses. By the time she began brushing them down, Alyse came over to help. Afterward, they greedily devoured the pies and drank the beer. Then they laid their cloaks on the ground and stretched out on them, thankful for the warmth of the afternoon sun.

Alyse fell asleep instantly . . .

And was awoken by Kate shaking her shoulder. "Get up!"

Alyse's heart leaped in panic. "W-what?"

"We overslept. It's almost evening."

Blinking to sharpen her focus, Alyse spotted the sun drifting down toward the horizon and turning the sky into a pale orange.

"We need to get going," Kate said.

After saddling the horses, Alyse and Kate resumed their journey. They traveled all night, the soft moonglow lighting their way like a constant beacon as they trotted through sleeping hamlets, villages, and towns. When dawn broke, the cousins stopped to rest and eat. Then they remounted and kept going all morning and into the afternoon, taking short breaks and stopping once in a town to buy food.

In the evening, they happened upon a large, two-story inn by a crossroads near an ancient red oak. In the faltering daylight, the sign swaying in the warm, gentle breeze said Red Oak Inn. The unshuttered windows glowed with friendly lamplight, and a plume of smoke curled up lazily from one of the two chimneys until it faded into the darkening sky. Several horses were hitched to iron rings set in stone blocks, and a few wagons were parked near the stable beside the inn, their horses waiting patiently in their traces. Music, singing, and laughter drifted out through the unshuttered windows.

"This place looks cheery enough," Alyse said. "Let's stay here tonight. Besides, I can't go any farther."

"Neither can I," Kate said.

As the girls dismounted, a boy with freckles—he couldn't have been older than twelve—who was standing outside the stable door, ran up to them and asked if they'd like him to take care of their horses. Kate handed him some coppers and instructed him to feed and brush down their mounts. After wiping the road dust from their clothes, the cousins put on their cloaks, slung their bulging saddlebags over their shoulders, and went into the inn.

The large common room was bustling with activity. Trestle tables were occupied by all sorts of commoner travelers, from merchants to farmers to wayfarers. A wandering bard stood near the unlighted hearth, strumming a mandolin and singing a rousing song. Some guests were singing along with her, waving their beer mugs in time to the music, while others were talking boisterously or focused on eating or simply listening. Many of the women and men clustered around the square tables along the walls ignored the commotion, preferring to chat among themselves.

Opposite the front door, a heavyset man in a soiled apron worked behind a counter that ran half the length of the room. He filled ceramic beer mugs and wine goblets from a bank of wooden barrels and handed them to customers at the bar or to a teenage serving girl to bring to the tables. The people at the counter appeared to be regulars because they bantered good-naturedly with the man, whom they called Deek. A sharp-faced woman came out of a door by the staircase to the second floor carrying two wooden trenchers full of stew, topped with thick slabs of bread, and headed toward a table.

"Is that man, Deek, the innkeeper or just a servant?" Alyse whispered to Kate. "I've never been to an inn before."

"How would I know?" Kate whispered back. "I've never been to one, either."

Inhaling deeply to settle her jittery nerves, Alyse walked up to Deek. "Are you the innkeeper?"

Putting his elbows on the counter, Deek leaned toward Alyse, his gaze taking in her plain commoner clothes. His eyes lingered for a moment on her sword and dagger partially hidden beneath her cloak, and then skipped over to Kate to check her out. "I am."

Alyse wrapped her cloak closer to her body to conceal her weapons. "Ya got a room for two? A private one." She cringed inwardly at her poor attempt to sound like a commoner. She'd never tried imitating their speech patterns before. And neither had Kate, who was brought up speaking like the noblesse.

The trace of a smile plucked at the corners of Deek's lips. "A private room for two, huh?"

"Yeah."

Deek stroked the sides of his mouth with a thumb and forefinger. "Just so happens I got one private room left."

"We'll take it," Alyse told him. "Your stableboy's already tendin' to our horses. We want supper too. What ya got for food?"

"Stew. Stew. Or stew."

Alyse couldn't hide her disappointment. She didn't like stew. "That's all?"

"Bread comes with it. Is there anything else you'd like?"

"A bath. Have two tubs taken up to our room. We wanna bathe before eating."

"This here is a *public* inn," Deek said, amusement in his voice. "The washrooms with tubs are communal. One for women. One for men. You take your baths there or stay dirty."

"All right. How much?"

Deek fingered his stubbly chin again, calculating. "Let's see now. Private room for two. Baths for two, including soap and towels. Supper and breakfast for two. Stabling two horses for one night." Deek named a price, which Alyse knew was much too high. He smirked at her, a challenge in his brown eyes.

Futile anger burned in Alyse because she knew he wouldn't budge. "Very well." She nodded to Kate. "Pay the man."

Kate took the money from her belt purse and handed the coins to Deek.

He pocketed them, then leaned across the bar, putting his face so close to Alyse's she could smell his bad breath. He spoke in almost a whisper. "A word of caution. The two of you might be dressed like commoners. And you did a fair job of talkin' like one. But ya gotta work on your el-lo-cution more. Here's a tip. Only a noblesse has her servant hold her money and pay the bills."

"My mother's a merchant," Alyse said sharply.

Deek handed Alyse a wry smile. "Maybe. But she didn't teach you no common sense. You don't display a heavy purse in a public place. That can prove dangerous for two young girls traveling by themselves, even if one is a backwatcher. There're brigands in the area. If I was you, I'd go get myself an armed escort."

"I'll keep that in mind. Now we'd like to go to our room." Alyse held out her hand. "The key."

"Key?" Deek guffawed and slapped the counter, causing nearby patrons to glance at him. He leaned toward Alyse again and spoke softly. "Here's another tip. To further your ed-u-cation. Public inns have common sleeping rooms, which ain't got no locks. But I can tell that you're used to fancier ways than us common folk. So I gave ya the one room that can be barred from the inside. When you're in the room, I suggest ya keep the door barred at all times."

"Thank you," Alyse said. "I'll keep that in mind."

Deek summoned the serving girl, who led them upstairs and down a dim hallway, which had windows at either end, to the next-to-last door on the left. Weak light from the setting sun filtering through the unshuttered window barely lit the room. The furnishings were plain and simple. A bed large enough to sleep three people. A nightstand on either side, each with an oil lamp. A clean chamber pot. A washstand with a bowl, a pitcher of water, soap, and towels. And pegs along a wall for hanging clothes. The single window looked out onto the stable and the woods beyond. There was no fireplace, and Alyse thanked the Goddess that they were traveling during First Fruits instead of the colder seasons of Reaping, Sleeping, or Awakening.

Kate closed the door while Alyse lit a lamp using flint and steel. "It's almost a two-week trip to your uncle's camp. But a few more nights at inns with prices like this one, and we'll be broke before we reach it."

"I know," Alyse said glumly.

"And only the Weavers know what other expenses we'll have to pay for before we get there."

"Like food."

"Maybe we should spend the nights in the woods from now on."

"Or try harder to pass ourselves off as commoners," Alyse said quickly. "We can work at it. Perhaps starting with our e-lo-cution."

She and Kate giggled.

"That'll take some doing," Kate said.

"We can practice while we're bathing."

After their baths, Alyse and Kate put on their extra set of clothes and went to the common room to eat. They found an empty table in a corner and sat across from each other.

The serving girl brought them wooden trenchers of chicken stew with slices of wheat bread on top and ceramic goblets of watered red wine. While they were eating, anxiety crawled up Alyse's spine on spidery legs because she sensed that she and Kate stuck out in the noisy room, like a pair of signal beacons. Whenever she glanced furtively around, though, everyone appeared to be more interested in the bard's songs or in their own conversations or food and drink than in two teenagers eating chicken stew.

After chatting for a while, Alyse and Kate turned their attention to the minstrel who was singing about two ill-fated lovers whose families were dead set against their marrying. Alyse wished she had a lover who would defy his family to marry her instead of having to flee a prospective husband who wanted to make her his wife against her will. Tuning out the bard's words, Alyse imagined what her lover would be like—

Kate touched Alyse's arm, then grinned and laughed as if Alyse had said something funny.

Alyse gave her an odd look, puzzled by Kate's bizarre behavior. "What—"

"Don't look now," Kate said, still grinning but her voice tense. "Two men at a table behind you have been eyeing us for some time now."

Alyse's shoulders turned into gooseflesh, but she managed to giggle back at Kate. "Do you recognize them?"

"No," Kate said, laughing. "One's wearing an eye patch, and the other has pockmarks all over his face. Ugh! They're definitely not anyone we want to know."

"Do you think they mean trouble?"

Kate grinned. "Well, they definitely seem interested in us. Let's finish eating and go up to our room. But don't hurry. And whatever you do, don't look at them. Let them think we haven't noticed."

At Kate's first words, Alyse's appetite had vanished. But she forced herself to continue eating, leisurely spooning her now-tasteless stew into her mouth. When she and Kate finished, they returned to their chamber. Kate barred the door.

"We'll leave first thing in the morning," Alyse said, "before breakfast. If those men mean trouble, we'll be long gone before they wake up."

Alyse and Kate climbed into bed fully clothed, leaving only their boots on the floor, and slipped their unsheathed daggers under their pillows. Despite the anxiety that looped around her like the coils of a snake, Alyse—exhausted from two days of travel—quickly fell into a deep, dreamless sleep.

And all too soon, Kate shook Alyse's shoulder. "It's time to go."

Alyse yawned and stretched. Through the thin walls on either side came sounds of snoring. Golden light from a rising dawn trickled through the window. Kate buckled on her sword belt. Then she and Alyse slung their saddlebags over their shoulders, picked up their boots, and quietly stole along the corridor and down the stairs on stockinged feet. Sounds of someone working in the kitchen filtered through the closed door. The front door was barred. Kate quietly lifted the heavy oak plank from the slats, and they stepped outside into the warm morning air.

The happy chirping of birds in the branches of nearby birch, elm, and poplar trees welcomed them. Alyse studied the trees and bushes, searching for telltale signs of the two men. Quick movement among some birch trees caught her attention. Her heart stopped. And then beat again when a fox trotted into view with a squirrel in its mouth.

Alyse sent a triumphant smile to Kate as they pulled on their boots. "We gave them the slip."

When they reached the stable, Kate opened one of the doors partway, and they sidled through the gap. Fortunately, the door to the hayloft was open, allowing enough amber sunlight inside for the girls to see. Alyse hastily saddled and bridled her mare and tied her saddlebags into place, then led the horse out of the stall.

Kate emerged from the adjoining stall at the same time. "I'll open the door all the way," Kate said, handing her reins to Alyse.

Before Kate could take a step, a hand gripped the partially open door and opened it wider.

Kate's hand dropped to her sword.

Two men came through the gap. They wore expensive but well-worn clothes. The taller man wore an eye patch. The shorter man had a pock-marked face and hefted a battle-ax menacingly.

"Well, well," Eye Patch said. "The chickens are flyin' the coop."

The men stepped forward a few paces.

Drawing her sword and dagger, Kate placed herself in front of Alyse.

Just then, several more women and men came through the doorway and fanned out on either side of Eye Patch and Pock Face. They were dressed in what looked like discarded, threadbare trappings of noblesse and noblesse commoners. They were armed with various weapons.

Pock Face hefted his battle-ax. "A backwatcher. As soon as I seed them two girlies last night, I knowed one was noblesse and the other her back-watcher."

Eye Patch's lips curved up into an unpleasant grin. "The little noblesse'll fetch us a tidy sum."

"Run!" Kate hissed. "Go out the back while I keep them busy."

Alyse drew her dagger. "Not without you."

"Don't be a fool. Flee!"

Two brigands—a man and a woman—sprang at Kate with their swords. She parried their blades, and the three of them danced back and forth across the floor planks, fighting. Instead of helping their two companions, the others watched the three fight as if they were observing a sports contest instead of a desperate life-or-death struggle. When the man stumbled away wounded, two of the onlookers replaced him.

"That's right," Eye Patch said. "Wear her out. She might be young, but she won't last forever."

"Tag-team match," Pock Face said, laughing gruffly.

Eye Patch sneered at Alyse, then nodded at a brigand and said, "Time to take the golden goose."

The man walked toward Alyse. The smirk on his lips told her he thought Alyse was easy prey. When he reached for her, she slipped under his arm and thrust her dagger into his side. He stumbled away, clutching the wound.

"She stabbed me! The little bitch stabbed me!" Then his eyes rolled up in his head and he collapsed. Blood flowed from his side, painting the floorboards red.

Alyse charged the brigands who were fighting Kate. She knifed one in the back.

With a shout, the brigands on the sidelines raced toward her.

She spun around to face them, but someone came up from behind and put his arm around her throat. Another seized the wrist of the hand holding the knife and squeezed. Alyse struggled, but the arm around her neck cut off her air, and the fingers pressing her wrist felt like the jaws of a vise. Her hand opened unwillingly, and the dagger clattered onto the pine planks.

Unsheathing his dagger, Eye Patch approached Alyse, grabbed and twisted a handful of her long chestnut hair, and jerked her head back. He positioned the blade against her throat.

Alyse dared not move or breathe while her heart slammed against her chest, like a prisoner trying to break out of jail.

"Drop your weapons, girlie," he called to Kate. "Or I'll slit her throat. Your matriarch won't like that, eh?"

Kate's opponents stepped back out of sword range. Kate looked toward Eye Patch, keeping her sword and dagger up.

Eye Patch drew the blade lightly across Alyse's neck. Blood dribbled down her neck, staining the front collar of her white linen shirt red. He leered at Kate. "Want more blood?"

He positioned his knife to make a deeper cut.

Kate threw down her sword, her face a combination of anger and disgust.

"And the dagger."

The knife clunked onto the planks.

Two brigands seized Kate by the arms. Dagger in hand, a third walked up behind her, grabbed a handful of her black hair, and yanked her head back to expose her neck. Then the woman placed the blade just below Kate's Adam's apple and shot Eye Patch a questioning look.

Eye Patch nodded. "Kill her."

CHAPTER 2

Pursuit

RILL LARKIN SQUINTED AT the late-afternoon sun while his gray gelding drank its fill from the trough near the inn. Frustration grabbed him in a choke hold. They had spent most of the day plodding along the road with the hot First Fruits season sun blazing down on them and hadn't covered much distance. Yet it was obvious—to him anyway—that Alyse and Kate Dejune were heading for The Marches in the east where Alyse's uncle, Leoc Dejune, was encamped with his legions.

Why couldn't Troy Estati admit that and head straight for The Marches, too, instead of insisting on stopping at every bloody hamlet, village, and town they came upon to ask if anyone had seen the girls passing through? Rill snorted to himself. Troy probably was doing it because he wasn't much of a rider and had a sore butt. None of them were experienced riders, except for himself. They could have traveled a lot farther if they hadn't dawdled.

Rill turned his gaze to the inn were Troy and his backwatcher, Yall Throwstarr, were inside asking if anyone had spotted the girls as a new thought struck his mind. *Failure.* Maybe Troy was so frightened of failing that he was setting himself up to do just that. *If it was me, I'd ride straight through till we caught up with 'em.*

Beside him, Livia Estati finished watering her horse—a bay-roan mare whose high spirits matched hers—led it to the hitching rings by the inn, and secured the mare next to Jade Channer's horse. Putting a hand on her buttocks, Livia arched her back and walked stiffly to Rill, using her mage's staff as a cane.

"My backside's killing me from riding that horse!" Livia wagged a finger under Rill's nose. "Slap me if I ever insist on doing something like this again."

So you'd leave your little brother to go with this bunch by himself. The chiding thought—made in jest—longed to escape from Rill's mouth as words. But he couldn't say them because his and Livia's blood relationship was a secret known only to the Estati adults. Despite his dislike of Troy, Rill's conscience squirmed uncomfortably because Troy wasn't privy to the secret. Troy still believed Livia was his sister.

Rill smiled at her and for the first time realized how soft and pampered the noblesse were, including his newly discovered half sister. Many noblesse walked within the walls of Caldon but refused to venture too far outside on foot. Some insisted on using litters inside the city, even to go to the public square when, in fact, walking would get them there faster. When traveling to their country villas, most went by litter and sometimes by wagon. And those few who went on horseback kept at a leisurely pace. Despite his political and magical powers, Deuth Estati, an archmage, was just as soft and pampered as the rest. The disparaging thought about his mentor and Livia's uncle caused a twitch of guilt in Rill because it seemed like he was being disloyal. And disloyalty toward Lord Deuth was one quality Rill refused to consider.

Rill shot Livia a playful smile. "For me, this has been an easy ride. One for beginners."

Livia rolled her dark blue eyes skyward. "That's because you're a country bumpkin."

Earlier, Rill would have considered her retort an insult. And perhaps it would have been. But Deuth's revelation about the mother Rill and Livia shared in common had resulted in a tectonic shift that had changed everything between Deuth's apprentice mage and his niece. Their shared secret was known only to the older generations of noblesse and commoners. Rill suppressed a smile. Anyone who wasn't in on the secret would have seen the playful banter between the two teenagers as a noblesse denigrating a commoner.

"Maybe it's just that I'm the better rider," Rill said, mischievousness lacing his words.

Livia performed another eye roll.

Rill slid his blue-eyed gaze to Jade Channer who was standing by the circular water fountain. She wore the distinctive Dejune livery of a tan light wool tunic with red trim around the neck, cuffs, and bottom and tan pants tucked into black boots. Like many female backwatchers, she wore her dark-brown, shoulder-length hair in a ponytail. He'd expected her to give some sort of reaction to Livia's supposed insult—perhaps a flicker in her hazel eyes or a twitch at the corner of her lips to signal a quickly suppressed snicker. Instead, she took a long swig from her canteen, pushed in the wood stopper, wrapped the leather strap around the pommel of her saddle, and then wiped an arm across her sweaty forehead. Maybe the Dejune backwatcher was paying more attention to the aches in her body than to the chitchat between him and Livia. Or possibly there was another reason. Jade had been broody ever since they'd left Caldon early that morning, giving Rill the impression she was an unwilling member of their little band of pursuers.

A short distance away, Magnus Roeback approached yet another local to ask if he'd seen two teenage girls passing through town yesterday. Magnus, a warrior mage who wore the black, purple-trimmed tunic and black pants and boots that marked him as an Estati backwatcher, had begun questioning locals in the street after Troy and Yall had disappeared into the inn. So far, everyone Magnus had stopped had complied instantly. And who wouldn't when confronted by a tall gray-haired mage in Estati livery who was traveling with two noblesse teens and two other backwatchers, one in Dejune livery and the other—Rill himself—wearing Estati livery?

Pride swelled Rill's chest as he tapped the butt of his staff against the dirt road. *But I ain't no backwatcher. I'm Lord Deuth's apprentice mage.*

Rill's attention snapped back to the inn as Troy and Yall emerged onto the dusty street and approached the water trough. Troy wore a discouraged expression as everyone gathered around the leader of their "rescue" operation. Troy ran his fingers through his reddish-brown hair as if he wanted time to pull together his thoughts.

Yall stood silently beside Troy, his black eyes cold and calculating as they swept across his companions and came to rest on Troy, waiting. Watching him, Rill always had the feeling that Yall examined people as if they were insects to be studied.

"The innkeeper didn't see them," Troy finally said, his voice betraying a note of frustration. "And no one else did, either."

Livia appeared to be the only one who seemed happy about Troy's announcement.

"Someone did." Magnus's lips formed a triumphant grin. "And I just spoke to him."

Everyone's eyes jumped to the middle-aged mage, who jerked a thumb at the forest farther up the road. "They headed into *that* last evening. It's called Malagnar Forest. And it's infested with brigands. He said he warned the girls about riding through it at night and suggested they spend the night here at the inn. But they refused."

"Then what are we waiting for?" Rill said. "Let's go after them while there's still daylight."

The others stared at him as if he had just said something idiotic.

Rill blew out an impatient breath. "Come on! We're wasting time."

"Are you insane?" Troy said, his tone indicating he already knew the answer. "The man said the forest's crawling with bandits."

Rill waved Troy's words aside as if he were swatting a fly. "So what? It ain't nothin' we can't handle."

Troy's jaw tensed. "You *are* crazy."

"Look," Rill said. "We got one bladeswoman, one bladesman, two mages, and me. I can cast spells, plus use a sword and a longbow. No one in her right mind would take on a group this strong."

"And you've got me too," Livia chimed in.

Rill loved her pluckiness. "Umm . . . no offense, Livia—"

"*Lady* Livia to you," Troy said.

"Lady Livia. And I don't mean to belittle your kind of magic. But you're an illusionist. I don't see how illusions can help in a fight."

Troy cut Livia off before she could reply. "That's a moot point because we're staying here tonight."

"Just because of a few brigands?" Rill said, striving to conceal his disdain.

"Because there's more than 'just brigands' in that forest," Troy said. "There are animals there too. Wild ones."

A snicker burst out of Rill's mouth before he could stop it. "Wild animals?" He dismissed the notion in a puff of breath. "They're more scared of us than we are of them." His gaze hopped like a bouncing ball from one face to another, reading fear in their eyes. Disdain rumbled in his chest. City folk! But he knew better than to say the disparaging words aloud.

"I'll go with you." Livia lobbed a challenging look at the others. "Anyone else willing to come along?"

"*I'm* in charge here," Troy said, clipping each word. "We're staying at the inn."

"That makes sense, actually," Magnus said in that reasonable tone Rill was beginning to dislike. "If the girls had the misfortune of being captured by brigands, there might be indications of it on the road." He pointed his mage's staff at Rill. "Lord Deuth said you can read signs. If the girls *were* captured, we'd miss those signs at night, wouldn't we?"

Rill cringed at the prospect of being showed up in front of Troy, but he had to concede Magnus's point. "Yeah. Probably."

"Then it's decided," Troy said, shooting a smirk at Rill. "We'll stay here tonight."

The next morning, they left right after breakfast. They traveled along the road through the dense forest at a slow trot, their horses' hooves kicking up small puffs of dry dirt. While they jogged along, a delicious sense of superiority filled Rill as he watched the fearful way the others gazed at the seemingly sinister screens of bushes and trees that hemmed them in on both sides and the partial roof of branches and leaves that arched overhead. He struggled to conceal his grins at the way they appeared to expect vicious, snarling animals to leap out at any moment.

"There ain't nothin' to be scared of in here," he told Livia quietly during their first rest stop. "Not as long as I'm with you."

All the while, Rill studied the road and the foliage on both sides for signs. It wasn't long after their second rest stop that he found some. He dismounted and studied them. What they told him made his muscles tighten.

"Something happened here," Rill said, pointing at a confusion of hoofprints on the road. A few were legible, while most had been partially obliterated by other hoofprints. "A lot of horses were here." He crossed to a wide gap in the bushes on the left side of the road and studied the ground.

"Horses were here. Four. Maybe five. Probably brigands lying in wait for victims." He went across to a trampled-down section of bushes on the other side. "Some waited here too."

Troy leaned in the saddle toward Rill, reddish-brown brows knitted together. "Then brigands did capture the girls."

"Don't know." Rill pointed farther up the road. "More tracks. They indicate a chase." He swung back onto his saddle. "Let's go see."

Rill led them at a moderate walk, his eyes studying the road while anxiety squeezed his chest tighter and tighter. Finally, he drew rein. His companions did the same and gathered around him.

"Well?" Troy said, cupping his hands on his saddle pommel and leaning toward Rill.

"They escaped." Rill indicated two sets of hoofprints heading up the road at full gallop, then at a jumble of prints their own horses were standing on. "And the brigands stopped here."

"Thank the One Goddess!" Livia said. "They're safe."

"As far as we know," Rill responded, worry still churning in his stomach. "That man said this forest is *infested* with brigands. So there's probably more than one group operating here."

The concerned look that crept onto Livia's face made Rill wish he hadn't given voice to his own fear.

Rill's anxiety about Alyse and Kate's possible capture by another band of brigands dissipated by the time they left Malagnar Forest because he hadn't found any other traces on the road pointing to bandits. He noticed that his companions appeared more at ease too. Especially Troy and Livia.

The new landscape they trotted through was more friendly than the forest, consisting of open, rolling grasslands and hills and a scattering of woods. It was a countryside studded with small farms—and some large ones—sitting on tilled land sprouting rows of ripening crops and pastures dotted with grazing cows, sheep, and goats. At one point, the little cavalcade followed alongside a murmuring stream lined with oak, birch, and spruce trees—some with fallen limbs poking out of the water—until it veered off in another direction. They also encountered crossroads. Troy hesitated at each one, as if unsure of himself, before continuing east toward The Marches.

In the late afternoon, when an inn came into sight, Troy announced that they would stop there. Rill argued that they should keep going. "We still got some daylight left, he said. "And Lord Deuth told us we gotta catch up with the girls before they reach Commander Dejune's camp."

"We'll stay at the inn," Troy said.

"Why? There ain't no forest to go through like last night."

"We're staying at the inn," Troy said, brows furrowed and an edge in his voice.

"Spend the night here if you want, Little Brother," Livia said. "But I'm going with Rill." She turned her mare's head up the road. "I see now why it's the women who rule Caldon. Because the men are too timid." She nodded at Rill. "Let's go."

"Wait!" Troy called out before Livia could press her heels against her mare's flanks. "We'll go. But we stop at the next inn we find."

They came upon "the next inn" during a magnificent sunset of reds, oranges, and yellows and set out again the next morning. To Rill's increasing frustration, Troy followed yesterday's routine of pausing at even the tiniest hamlet they passed through to inquire about the girls. But Rill kept his teeth clamped down around his tongue. He'd complained enough yesterday to earn Troy's ire and didn't want to get him even more riled up today. Fortunately, Magnus suggested they pass through the hamlets without pausing to ask about Kate and Alyse.

"The girls are more likely to have stopped in a village or town instead of a hamlet to buy food for themselves and feed for their horses," Magnus said. "The hamlets are smaller and tend to be suspicious of strangers. So let's bypass them and focus on the villages and towns to ask our questions."

Grudgingly, Troy agreed.

Magnus's advice paid off. That afternoon, when they asked about the girls, in a cozy little town by a crossroads, they learned that two teenagers matching Alyse's and Kate's descriptions had bought meat pies, beer, and grain feed there the previous afternoon.

"They have a day's lead on us," Magnus said, fingering the silver ring on his left earlobe. "That shows they're traveling hard—"

"Or we're traveling too slow," Rill said, not masking his impatience.

Magnus ignored the comment. "We'll have to travel hard, too, if we want to catch up with them before they reach The Marches."

"Let's stop wasting our time stopping to ask questions," Rill said. "Lady Alyse and Kate got their food. So there ain't no need for them to buy more for a while. And I got a hunch they slept outdoors last night."

Jade disagreed. "I believe we're closer than we think because they probably stayed at an inn last night, not outdoors. Lady Alyse is used to the soft life."

Rill shook his head stubbornly. *Jade don't know Alyse at all.* "She ain't soft. Which is obvious 'cause they turned a half-day's lead into a full day's. Like Magnus said, they're traveling hard. Which means they're probably sleeping outdoors." He hurled a malicious grin at Troy. "In the woods."

Troy returned the look with a scathing one.

They spent that night at another inn and left before the serving girl could clear the dirty dishes from their breakfast table. Late in the day, they came upon a quaint inn at a crossroads near a huge, ancient red oak tree.

"How appropriate," Jade said dryly when she read the name on the sign hanging over the inn's door: Red Oak Inn.

While they were climbing out of their saddles, a young freckle-faced boy raced out of the stable and offered to take their horses. While the others went inside the inn, Rill accompanied the lad to the stable, leading three of their horses to help out. Inside, he let the boy curry the others' horses but insisted on grooming his own to make sure the job was done right. Afterward, as he slung his quiver over his shoulder and picked up his staff, the bag containing his longbow, and his saddlebag, he noticed the boy sneaking wide-eyed glances at the longbow bag. Smiling to himself at the kid's fascination, he went into the inn to join the others. He found Magnus in a heated conversation with a stocky man behind the bar wearing a dirty apron. Rill figured he must be the innkeeper. Livia, Troy, and the others stood a short distance away, watching. The frown on Troy's face kept deepening.

"I don't care if the two rooms are taken," Magnus said. "We want them for the night."

"The guests have already paid for them," the man said.

"What's your name again?"

"Deek."

Magnus grabbed Deek's arms near the shoulders and half pulled him over the bar. "Listen, Deek. Do you see the livery I'm wearing?"

"Y-yeah."

Releasing Deek, Magnus pointed to Rill and Yall. "And theirs?"

Deek nodded.

"Black with purple trim. Ring any bells?"

Deek's jaw dropped open as if on oiled hinges, and his face paled. "Estati!"

Magnus grinned at Deek. "Give the man a mug of his best! Yes. Estati. Now, tell me. Do you really want to anger our matriarch because you denied us rooms? After all, her arm has a long reach. Even to here."

Deek's Adam's apple bobbed as he gulped down a huge mouthful of saliva. "N-no. Of course not."

Magnus patted Deek on the cheek. "Smart man. Give the people back their money. If they have questions, they can speak to me."

As Deek made to leave, Troy grabbed his arm. "I'm looking for two girls traveling by themselves. One's petite. Long, chestnut hair. Emerald-green eyes. Brown eyebrows. The other's taller. Black hair. Hazel eyes. Wiry build. Have you seen them?"

Deek's eyebrows shot up. "Yeah. They spent the night here."

"When?" Magnus asked.

"Night before last. They left yesterday just before breakfast."

"Which way did they go?"

Deek shrugged. "Don't know. No one saw 'em leave."

Magnus turned to Troy, his silver eyes shining with triumph. "This is the first time they've stayed at an inn. That means they think they must have a good lead on us. If we ride hard tomorrow, we'll cut down their lead and maybe even catch up with them sometime the day after."

Excitement rippled across Rill's shoulders. They were closing in!

Jade grinned. "Well before they reach The Marches."

Troy pressed his lips into a determined line. "Tomorrow we ride as hard as we can. No stragglers."

The next morning after breakfast, Magnus told Deek to tell the stableboy to saddle their horses and bring them to the hitching posts. Rill preferred to saddle his own horse himself instead of entrusting it to a young boy he didn't know. So, after gathering his staff, weapons, and saddlebag, he walked to the stable. The stableboy was tightening the girth on Livia's mare, and Rill noted approvingly that the lad knew what he was doing. After he saddled his gelding, Rill was about to attach the bow bag to the saddle when he noticed the boy eyeing the bow bag again. Rill smiled at the kid. "What's your name?"

"Dane, Lord."

Rill chuckled, inwardly pleased that the boy had mistaken him for noblesse. *Not yet, anyways.* "I ain't no lord."

Dane's eyes latched on to the bow bag again.

"Ever shoot a longbow?" Rill asked.

Dane shook his head.

"Ever want to?"

"Yeah!" Dane let out a discouraged sigh. "But my dad . . . he says I ain't got no time for such foolishness. 'Cause I gotta work. Besides, I'm too young to use a longbow. The draw weight's too strong."

"You ain't too young," Rill responded with a smile. "I began using a longbow when I was seven."

"Really?"

"Yeah. My dad gave me one that had a draw weight I could handle."

"Wish my dad would."

"Wanna try mine?"

Dane's eyes lit up like a pair of lanterns. "Really?"

"Yeah."

Dane frowned. "But the draw weight—"

"Don't worry about that. You'll manage."

Rill slid the longbow out of its brown-cloth case, strung it, and slid an arrow from the leather quiver. He searched for a target while he nocked the arrow. "See that discoloration on the wood on the wall over there? The one the size of your fist?"

"Yeah."

In one deft motion, Rill drew and canted the bow and let fly the arrow. The broadhead struck dead center with a loud *thunk*.

Dane clapped his hands in delight.

Rill handed him the bow. "Now you try."

He gave Dane some pointers, but of course, the bow was too tall and the draw weight too heavy for the boy. So, standing behind him, Rill helped the lad shoot. The arrow, thanks to Rill, pierced the discoloration.

Dane shrieked in delight. "I shot a longbow!"

"And hit the mark too," Rill said, grinning.

The happy light in Dane's eyes suddenly dimmed, and his hand tightened on the longbow's leather-wrapped grip until the knuckles showed white. "If I'd knowed how to use this yesterday, I could of helped those ladies." Then he gasped in dismay and clapped a hand over his mouth.

A ball of anxiety formed in Rill's stomach. "What ladies?"

Dane dropped the longbow and backed away, his expression fearful as if Rill were an evil apparition from Shelar, the Underworld.

Rill stepped toward him, brow narrowed and eyes hard as blue diamonds. "What ladies?"

"I . . . I ain't supposed to tell. My dad . . . he said it would bring us trouble if I did."

Rill grabbed Dane by the front of his tunic and yanked him in close. "And I say it'll bring you trouble if you don't. So talk!"

"T-the two ladies who stopped here the night before last—"

"One with chestnut hair and the other with black hair?"

"Yeah."

"What happened to them?"

"Brigands. They took 'em."

The words felt like barbed arrows piercing Rill's chest. "How do you know that?"

"'Cause I watched 'em do it."

"You actually saw them being captured?"

"Yeah." Dane pointed to the hayloft. "I sleep up there. At least, when the inn's full and my dad's gotta let out my room, I do. Like two nights ago. The girls . . . they woke me up when they came in and saddled their horses. Then the brigands came in and took 'em away."

Snatching his staff, Rill spun around and dashed out of the stable and into the inn and past tables where travelers sat eating breakfast, his heart racing faster than his feet. He stopped short at the trestle table where Troy and the others were chitchatting over empty bowls and mugs.

"I just learned about the girls," Rill said, his voice low and urgent. "It's not good. Come with me."

Everyone jumped to their feet and followed Rill to the kitchen door. Rill tapped Yall on the chest. "Stay here and don't let anyone in. The rest of you, follow me."

Without waiting for a response, Rill barged through the door. In the kitchen a thin, middle-aged woman, with sharp features whose edges were beginning to dull, was kneading bread at a long, wide wooden preparation table while a teenage serving girl stirred the contents of a kettle hanging over the hearth flames. Deek, who was across the table from the woman, was lifting an earthenware mug to his mouth. Startled, all three glanced at the intruders in surprise.

Rill knocked the mug from Deek's hand with his staff, oblivious to the sound of it shattering on the floor. Then, dropping the staff and drawing his dagger, he grabbed the innkeeper by the shirt and wrenched him in close. He touched the tip of the dagger to Deek's throat. The point nicked the skin, drawing blood.

Deek jerked his neck back in terror.

Troy, Livia, Magnus, and Jade crowded around the two of them.

"You lying bastard," Rill said through teeth clenched so tight the words came out in a low, angry whisper. "You knew those girls didn't leave yesterday. At least, not by themselves. Brigands took them."

Livia put a hand to her throat. "Alyse and Kate were *kidnapped*?"

Troy, his face dark with unsuppressed fury, pulled his fist back to strike Deek in the face. "You son of a bitch!"

Magnus grabbed Troy's wrist. "I think the knife at his throat is doing nicely, Lord." He nodded at Rill. "What's this all about?"

"Alyse and Kate never left here," Rill said, his voice tight with anger. "At least not of their own free will."

Troy tilted his head, mystified. "What do you mean?"

"They were captured by brigands. In Deek's stable. The stableboy saw it all." Rill pressed the dagger point deeper into Deek's throat, increasing the dribble of blood, which slid down his neck and soaked into the collar of his brown tunic. "And this little piece of shit told him to keep quiet about it."

Taking hold of Rill's wrist, Magnus gently drew the knife hand back from Deek's neck. "I think a dead innkeeper won't be of much value to us right now. You can kill him later if you want."

Rill released Deek's shirt with a shove toward the preparation table. Deek struck the table edge, then sank onto his knees. Troy stepped up to him, the toes of his black leather boots almost touching Deek's kneecaps. Deek clasped his hands together, imploring. "Oh, Lord, please don't—"

Troy kicked him in the stomach. With a shriek of pain, Deek clutched his belly and doubled over so his forehead struck the floorboards. He flopped onto his side and groaned.

Troy towered over him, glowering. "You fat little piece of horseshit. I'm betrothed to one of those girls."

Troy brought his foot back for another kick, but Livia pressed herself between him and Deek. "Beating him to death won't help us rescue the girls." She looked down at the groaning innkeeper. "Why didn't you tell us the truth before?"

"'Cause if the brigands learned I'd told you," Deek said, the words wheezing from his mouth, "they'd take it out on me and my family. Maybe even kill us."

An angry rumble sounded in Troy's throat. He reached down to yank Deek to his feet, but Livia batted his arm aside and knelt in front of the innkeeper.

Then she took a white linen handkerchief from her sleeve and pressed it against Deek's still-trickling neck wound. "Is that true?" she asked.

Deek put his hand on the handkerchief, forcing it against the wound as Livia removed hers. "Yeah."

Troy motioned to Magnus. "Get the kid in here."

"Please, Lords—no!" the woman said, moving around the table and kneeling beside Deek. "Our son meant no harm."

Magnus arched his brow questioningly at Troy, who nodded.

Rill glanced at the serving girl huddling fearfully in a corner and recalled the sincerity of Dane's desire to help Alyse and Kate. "Ain't no need to get the kid involved. He can't add nothin'."

The woman flashed him a grateful look. "For the love of the One Goddess," she said, "have pity on us. The brigands . . . they got a camp somewhere in the hills nearby. If they find out we told you about them taking the girls . . . My husband spoke the truth. They'll murder us and burn down the inn."

"That's the Goddess's own truth," Deek said as he struggled into a sitting position with his back against a table leg. "I beg you, Lords. Think of my son and daughter. Those bastards will kill me and my wife and take my kids as slaves."

Troy's lips curled into a snarl. "Not if we kill 'those bastards' first."

"There're too many of 'em, Lord," the wife said. "And there's mages among them."

"Rohan!" Magnus muttered.

Troy prodded Deek with the toe of his boot. "Where's their camp?"

"In the hills."

"*Where* in the hills?"

"I don't know."

Troy pulled his leg back for another kick, but Livia, who was still kneeling beside Deek, blocked his ankle with her hand. She spoke to Deek. "You'd tell us if you knew."

Deek nodded. "Yeah."

"No one knows its location but the brigands themselves," Deek's wife said. "And that's the Goddess's honest truth."

"How'd they learn the girls were here?" Rill asked.

"A couple of the brigands come here most nights. To look for victims to waylay."

"And you let them." Troy spat the words at her like arrows.

She thrust out her chin defiantly. "They'd kill us if we warned our visitors. We ain't got protectors and backwatchers like you."

Troy hurled her a look brimming with disgust.

"We warn 'em," Deek said quickly. "But it's up to them to take the hint." He began struggling onto his feet. Livia grabbed him under the shoulders and helped. Deek leaned back against the preparation table for support. "I warned the girls. Told 'em they should go back and get an armed escort."

Rill's brow crinkled as a plan formed in his head. "Will the brigands come here again tonight?"

Deek shrugged. "Don't know. Sometimes they come the very next night. Other times they wait a day or two. Maybe even more. They didn't come last night."

"Let's hope they come tonight," Rill said.

"What do you have in mind?" Troy asked.

"We'll capture them and make them take us to their camp."

"And what happens if they don't?" Magnus asked.

For the first time, Jade spoke up. "It might not make any difference one way or the other."

"Why?" Rill asked.

"Because they might already have killed Lady Alyse and Kate."

The expression on Jade's face told Rill she'd be happy if they had.

CHAPTER 3

Capture

"WAIT!" ALYSE CRIED, IGNORING Eye Patch's sharp blade at her throat. "I'm Alyse Dejune. Granddaughter of Chief Mage Jukka Berne. Niece of Leoc Dejune, Commander of the Eastern Legions. I'm betrothed to Troy Estati, whose great-grandfather was co-chief mage with my grandfather. That girl is my cousin, Kate Dejune. My family will pay a good ransom for both of us."

The woman holding the dagger at Kate's throat raised an inquiring eyebrow at Eye Patch.

The seconds crept by. Alyse's muscles tensed as she waited anxiously for Eye Patch's response.

"Let her live," Eye Patch said.

The woman resheathed her blade as Eye Patch removed his knife from Alyse's throat and let go of her hair. Alyse's shoulders sagged in relief as the tension gushed out of her body. She pressed her hand over her neck wound, feeling warm, wet blood on her palm.

Eye Patch pointed at the brigand Alyse had knifed who was lying on the pine floorboards. "Is he dead?"

A woman knelt to examine him. "Naw. He'll live."

"Bind up his wound and get him on a horse." Eye Patch jerked a thumb at Alyse. "And give the girlie here something for hers too."

Someone handed Alyse a soiled piece of linen he'd taken from inside the sleeve of his tunic. Alyse hid her disgust at the cloth's uncleanliness as she tied it in place.

Eye Patch slipped his dagger back into its scabbard, put his hands on his hips, and eyed Alyse as if he were a horse buyer sizing up the worth of a mare. Alyse returned his stare unflinchingly. She wouldn't let him intimidate her.

"Dejune, ya say? I know someone who'll be interested in meeting you."

"Who?" Alyse asked, unable to hide her curiosity.

Eye Patch's lips curled into a nasty smile. "Oh, I'll let that be a surprise."

The other brigands snickered in a way that sent an icy chill sliding down Alyse's back.

Eye Patch's smile morphed into a scowl. "Listen to me good, girlie. Your cousin here might be a high-an'-mighty Dejune like you. But if ya give us any trouble, it'll be bye-bye, Katie." His gaze shifted to the bronze chain around Alyse's neck. "You a mage?"

"Yes."

"What kind?"

"A healer." Alyse pointed with her chin to the man she had stabbed. "I should take a look at his wound."

Eye Patch shook his head.

"But it might get infected."

Eye Patch gave a short, dismissive laugh. "If he was stupid enough to let you stick him, he deserves the infection. Besides, we know how to treat knife wounds. Don't need no la-di-da noblesse healer for that." Eye Patch unclasped Alyse's bronze charm and jammed it into his belt purse. "You won't be needing this no more, neither."

After binding Alyse's and Kate's hands behind their backs, a couple of brigands boosted them up into the saddles of their mares and led the horses out of the stable and around to the back where the outlaws had tethered their own horses. Then they each drew a long length of rope from their saddlebags. Alyse's blood turned cold when she saw the noose tied at the end of each rope. The brigands put the nooses around the cousins' necks. The rough strands scratched Alyse's throat. Then, positioning their horses behind the girls' mares and holding the other ends of the ropes, the brigands climbed into their saddles.

"You try to escape," Eye Patch told the girls, then nodded at the two outlaws behind them, "they'll yank you out of your saddles and string you up to a tree limb . . . if our horses don't trample you first."

His threat made Alyse's heart pound painfully in her chest while a knot of dread about her and Kate's fates formed in her stomach.

Eye Patch rode in the lead, with Alyse and Kate trotting right behind him, and took the procession down the road a little way before veering off into green meadows, rolling hills, babbling rivers, and scrubby woods. At one point, they returned to the road—whether it was the same one they'd taken initially, Alyse couldn't tell—and went through a hidden passageway in the bushes. They loped along until midmorning. Alyse, though, got the impression they hadn't traveled a great distance. Instead, her captors appeared to be riding in circles to confuse her and Kate, probably so she and Kate wouldn't be able to lead Dejune protectors and backwatchers to the brigands' hideout after they were ransomed.

At last, they emerged from the woods at the crest of a low hill that looked down upon a grassy clearing surrounded by woods. A pair of ramshackle log cabins with stone chimneys sat on the far side, one large and the other about half its size. A well, with a wooden bucket beside it, was near the larger cabin. A sturdy shed partially filled the gap between the cabins with what appeared to be a two-door outhouse behind it, near the forest's edge. A long stack of split kindling that almost came up to Alyse's shoulders took up the space near the front of the shed on the left and, a few feet to the right, a pile of unsplit logs rose almost as high, creating a tunnel. A chopping block surrounded by wood chips stood just inside the entrance, the blade of a long-handled ax embedded in it. To the right of the wood stacks was a run-down stable whose weathered side formed the last part of a rectangular corral.

It seemed to Alyse that the brigands had been living there for quite some time.

She started when a woman suddenly emerged from behind a clump of bushes near Eye Patch. Gnarly light brown hair framed her tanned face. She appeared to be in her mid-twenties and wore matching dark-blue tunic and pants. Alyse could tell that the material had been expensive when new but now was grungy and patched, just like the other brigands' clothing. A sword and dagger were belted around her slim waist, and she carried a spear.

"Ya got 'em, I see," she said to Eye Patch.

Eye Patch grinned at her. "A bigger catch than expected." He jerked a thumb behind him at Alyse at and Kate. "Dejunes. Both of 'em. Far from their cozy home on The Citadel."

The woman's gaze flicked from Alyse to Kate, then returned to Eye Patch. Her lips spread into a nasty smile. "He'll be pleased."

Eye Patch belted out a laugh. "Ecstatic is more like it. Plus, with the ransom they'll bring, we'll be rich."

The knot in Alyse's stomach tightened as she wondered who "he" was and why he would be pleased Dejunes had been captured. She sneaked a peek at Kate to see her reaction, but her cousin was gazing stonily ahead. Snapping her green eyes forward, Alyse strove to ignore the knot, which kept twisting tighter and tighter. *You're a Dejune. Don't let them cower you.* She set her face into an expressionless mask as the small cavalcade of grubby brigands jogged down into the clearing, leaving the sentry behind.

Some women and men were playing a game of shoveball in front of the buildings while others were lounging on the porches. When they spotted their fellow brigands approaching, the shoveball players stopped their game, and the women and men on the porches stood up to watch the riders come in. Like their captors and the sentry, these brigands wore dirty, once-fine clothes as well.

"Hey, Larch!" Eye Patch called out. "Tell him we got 'em!"

A man standing on the porch of the larger cabin waved in acknowledgment, then opened the front door and shouted, "They're back!" Moments later, several brigands spilled out to join the others on the porch as Eye Patch drew rein in front of the cabin.

One of the brigands on the porch—a trim young woman with dark-brown, shoulder-length hair worn in a ponytail—drew Alyse's attention. A gasp escaped from Alyse's mouth when their eyes met, but the woman made no sign of recognition.

"Freya!" Alyse said. "It's me—"

"Shaddup!" The outlaw holding Alyse's rope jerked on it.

Alyse choked as the raspy hemp cut into her throat.

Standing in his stirrups, Eye Patch scanned the group. His gaze fell on the man who had shouted inside the cabin. "Call him again."

"*You* do it." The man's tone bordered on belligerence. "I ain't your servant."

"Humph!" Eye Patch cupped his hands around his mouth. "Hey, Palquo! I brought ya a couple of real nice gifts."

The name made Alyse's heart soar with relief. *Palquo! He'll let us go when he discovers who we are.*

A man in his late forties, whose head was topped with oily, dirty-blond hair, stepped through the doorway onto the porch, his back as stiff as the mage's staff he held. Beneath his thick, blond brows, his brown eyes appeared to be locked in a perpetual squint—a quirk Alyse remembered well. Like the others, his garments were expensive but worn.

"Palquo!" Alyse cried, relief washing over her like a tidal wave. "It's me. Alyse Dejune."

The brigand controlling her rope gave it another painful yank. "I said shaddup!"

Alyse almost toppled out of her saddle but recovered just in time. She focused her eyes on Palquo, positive he would set them free. But when Palquo's gaze met hers, his brown eyes were as cold as a pair of ice cubes. He said nothing, just watched in silence as the outlaws dismounted and then yanked Alyse and Kate out of their saddles.

"You could at least take these nooses off," Alyse said, unable to hide her indignation.

Her words were followed by a wrench on the rope that almost knocked her off-balance.

Palquo stepped to the edge of the porch.

Alyse couldn't keep an imploring tone from her voice. "Palquo, don't you recognize me? Alyse Deju—"

"Stupid girlie. Don't ya never listen? Shaddup!" Eye Patch knocked Alyse's legs out from beneath her with a swift kick. Her shoulder hit the ground hard, sending pain streaking down her arm.

The brigands watched mutely while she struggled onto her feet, which was an awkward task with her hands tied behind her back.

Keeping his eyes focused on Alyse, Palquo stepped off the porch onto the grass. When he finally spoke, bitterness saturated his words. "Of course I know who you are, Alyse Dejune. It was your grandmother who expelled me." He nodded at Freya. "And her." Then he pointed with his chin to someone in the group of outlaws standing behind her. "And him."

Alyse turned to see where Palquo was pointing. A young man partially concealed behind a pair of brigands stepped into full view. Alyse gasped in recognition. *Geoff!*

Kate was standing beside Alyse. She made a dismissive sound. "You said it yourself, Palquo. It was Lady Maude who expelled you, Freya, and Geoff. Not Lady Alyse. She had nothing to do with it."

"She's a *Dejune!*" Palquo spat the word as if it were a piece of rancid meat. "I—we—the three of us were expelled because we survived the surprise attack on their compound that night. Perhaps if we'd died along with the other defenders who fought alongside us, Lady Maude might have praised us. But we lived instead. So she condemned and expelled us."

Alyse's muscles went numb as the horrible scene replayed in her head. Freya, Geoff, and Palquo walking into the matriarch's chamber under armed guard and stopping by the steps leading up to the matriarch's chair where Grandmother Maude, the family's matriarch, sat gazing down on them like one of the Three Judges who determined the fates of the dead. The sole survivors of the small group of protectors who had initially defended the rear of the family compound when the attack had been sprung. Freya and Geoff standing before her, chins raised defiantly. Geoff's bitter words rose in Alyse's mind like haunting ghosts. "We had the misfortune of surviving. You're holding that against us out of spite." And Palquo on his knees, arms outstretched, begging for mercy. His plea reverberated in Alyse's mind. "Show mercy to me. Don't make me a rohan."

But Grandmother Maude had shown mercy to none of them. Instead, she had banished them not because they had survived but to set an example and also to protect a family secret: generations ago, the last Dejune archmage had cast wards on the door of the family's charm vault to keep their charms safe until another powerful archmage was born who could cancel them. But no mages, let alone an archmage, had been born since then. Until Alyse. And she had to keep her powers secret if she wanted to stay alive.

"I never blamed you," Alyse told Palquo. "I defended you. I stood up for Freya and Geoff too. Don't you remember?"

Palquo's voice lashed out at her like a whip. "You're a Dejune. That's all that matters."

"That's right, Palquo," Kate said in a tone saturated with scorn. "Let your hatred overcome your common sense."

Palquo strode up to Kate and slapped her hard across the face with the back of his hand. A blue sapphire ring on his middle finger cut a thin, bloody gash on her cheek. "And you're a Dejune too. Goddess damn you. Goddess damn you both!"

Freya hurried down the porch steps and placed a hand on Palquo's arm. "Lady Alyse always treated us kindly. And Kate is just a retainer like we were."

Palquo yanked free of her grip. "Kate's a Dejune."

"She was my sparring partner. Geoff's too. She's one of us."

Palquo's face turned dark as a storm cloud ready to burst into rain. "Dejune blood runs in her veins."

"No. Kate is one of us."

Palquo stepped toward her until their noses almost touched. His right eye twitched. "Who leads this band—you or me?"

Freya stepped back. "You."

His hard brown eyes glared. "Then don't oppose me. Kate is one of *them*."

Freya dropped her gaze and spoke meekly. "As you say, Palquo."

"Remember that the next time you think about defending a Dejune." Palquo motioned to Eye Patch. "Bring 'em inside."

The brigands shoved Alyse and Kate toward the stairs of the larger cabin, making them scurry onto the porch and through the door. The interior was spacious, lit by harsh sunlight streaming through four open-shuttered windows and by the flames of a fire crackling ominously in a hearth made of stones. The fire's heat combined with the warmth of the day made the place uncomfortably hot. A pair of iron pots hung from a crane over the flames. A girl in her mid-teens, a black eye and bruises marring what had once been a pretty face, replaced the lid on one of the kettles and cringed as the bandits entered.

A long trestle table and two benches occupied the center of the room. Mugs, dice, cards, and coins were scattered across the tabletop. In the stifling air, the aroma of a delicious stew made war against the stench of unwashed bodies.

Palquo motioned imperiously to the girl. "Bring us wine."

The girl scurried away to carry out his command.

The men with the ropes led Alyse and Kate to a clear space near the trestle table. When the girls stopped, the brigands formed a ring around them. Palquo stood inside the circle with the cousins. He studied them for a long time through hard, cruel eyes. Alyse, chin up, returned the stare with a defiant one.

"Well . . . well . . . well," Palquo said. "What are we to do with you?"

Eye Patch pointed to Alyse. "The girlie—"

Palquo cut him off sharply. "Show the bitch some respect. She's noblesse."

"Umm, sorry. The *noblesse* girlie said her family would pay a hefty ransom for her and her cousin."

Palquo gave a derisive snort. "Her family couldn't pay me enough gilders to make up for what they did to me. I think I'll send their fingers to their matriarch." He squinched his lips together, thinking. "Or maybe their heads."

Alyse's bladder suddenly felt full, and she fought against the urge to pee. His words were a threat, and nothing more. She hoped.

The brigands glanced uneasily at one another.

Eye Patch stepped into the empty space with Palquo, his brows dipped into a frown. "Revenge is fine. And we don't care what you do with the girlies—as long as we can make money off of 'em too."

The other brigands growled their agreement.

Alyse's heart quivered like a bird in its death throws while she struggled to control her bladder. Yet, somehow, she managed to keep her voice stern. "Palquo, my uncle is Commander of the Eastern Legions. If you harm me or Kate, he'll march his legions here and clean out this snake den of yours."

A concerned murmur rippled through the brigands as they traded apprehensive glances back and forth.

Palquo let out a hearty belly laugh as if she'd just said something hilarious. "You'll have to find a better threat to scare me with." He thrust his face so close to Alyse that she could smell his foul breath. "You know why? Because we're in Caldonian territory, and he can't leave The Marches." Palquo backed away and sniggered. "Besides, he'll never know what happened to you."

"She's right," a woman's voice said from somewhere in the back of the assembled bandits. "This is our chance to make more gilders than we ever dreamed possible. The girls are a gift to us from the One Goddess Herself. We'd be fools to reject it."

Voices muttered in agreement.

Palquo slammed the end of his staff on the rough floorboards. "I'm the leader here! I killed Malak. You all saw me do it. I took his place, and you all consented to it."

"'Cause the pickings Malak was givin' us was slim," someone behind Palquo shouted. "You promised to change that but haven't. These two girlies have given ya the chance to make good on your promise—or be replaced yourself."

Palquo spun toward the voice. "Who said that?" He turned slowly around the circle, his angry gaze darting from one brigand to another, but no one responded. Palquo snorted his disgust. "Too yellow to show yourself, eh?"

Pushing between two brigands, Pock Face stepped into the clear space and stopped beside Eye Patch. His hand rested on the head of the battle-ax stuck through his brown leather belt. "I said it."

"You think you can lead this band better than me?" Palquo asked, his voice dangerously calm.

Pock Face shook his head. "No. And I ain't got no desire to lead it, neither. I'm just sayin' that you promised us easier—and better—pickings than Malak gave us."

Murmurs of agreement rippled through the crowd of outlaws. Palquo started to respond, but Eye Patch cut him off. "We'll gain nothing from arguin' between ourselves. I call for a band meeting. It's my right as a member. We'll let the band vote on what to do with the girlies." He made a slow circle of the onlookers, his gaze sweeping across the faces. "What d'ya say, sisters and brothers?"

The brigands cheered their approval.

Eye Patch turned back to Palquo. "We're all in agreement. What d'ya say, brother?"

Alyse could tell by Palquo's sour expression that he was both surprised and angered by the unexpected turn of events. But he put on his best face by heaving an indifferent shrug. "Looks like I don't have a choice."

"D'ya promise to abide by our decision?"

"Yeah."

Then swear by the One Goddess."

Palquo's blond brows plunged into a scowl. "What—my word isn't good enough for ya?"

"Of course it is," Eye Patch said with a sly smile. "Which is why you shouldn't mind swearin'."

Palquo made his oath.

The slave girl had been hovering in the background with a large jug of wine in her hands. Now she stepped forward and offered the crock to one of the brigands, who held it up. "Let's drink, sisters and brothers," he said. "To plenty of gildas an' better times ahead!"

Cheering, the brigands snatched up mugs from the tables as the girl filled them up. The men holding the ends of Alyse's and Kate's ropes let them drop onto the pine floor and rushed to join their comrades. Freya hesitated, then started toward the throng.

Palquo stepped in front of her. "Not you." He took a key from his leather belt purse and handed it to her. "Since you defended them, you're responsible for them. Put them in the shed. Your life is forfeit if they escape."

Turning, he went to celebrate with the others.

Freya picked up the ropes and yanked them hard, nearly knocking Alyse and Kate off their feet. Then she snapped the ropes as if they were reins on horses, chafing Alyse's neck. "Come on," she said, forcing the captives toward the door.

CHAPTER 4

Unexpected Ally

OUTSIDE, FREYA ORDERED ALYSE and Kate to walk in front of her to the shed. When they reached it, Freya made Kate open the door, then shoved both cousins through the doorway with such force that they stumbled across the rough-hewn pine planks, lost their footing, and fell. Alyse landed on her back. She rolled over onto her stomach, got to her knees, and stood up. Kate regained her feet a few moments later.

Alyse took in her dingy surroundings. The shed was nine or ten staff lengths long and six or seven wide, and high enough for Freya—the tallest of the three—to stand upright. The rear and side walls each had a single un-shuttered window at shoulder level that allowed a stingy amount of sunlight inside. Alyse's heart quaked when she spotted several sets of iron manacles, each one consisting of two iron rings connected together by an iron chain. That chain was attached to a thicker one that was firmly anchored to the stout log walls.

"Hmm . . . nice place you got here," Kate said with feigned nonchalance.

Alyse nodded her agreement, her heart smashing against her rib cage while she strove to match her cousin's outward coolness. "Yes. Reminds me of home."

"You don't have to put on an act for me," Freya said.

Kate made a sudden move toward Freya.

Freya quickly backed away. Her hand grasped the leather-wrapped grip of her sword, ready to pull the weapon from its scabbard. "Kate, don't! If you give me trouble, I'll have to kill you."

Kate spat words at her. "You've become just like them."

Freya shook her head, making her ponytail swing, while a pained expression slid onto her face. "No I haven't. But if you give me too much trouble, I'll have to kill. And I don't want to."

Kate made a scoffing sound in her throat.

"I mean it." Freya glanced behind her as if she expected to find a brigand standing in the open doorway. Then, turning her eyes frontward, she spoke softly and quickly, each word chasing closely behind the other. "If you escape, they'll kill me. That's what happens if one of us 'caretakers' gets too chummy or careless with the hostages."

Alyse's heart cracked as she imagined the pain and stress Freya must feel in her role as their jailer. "Oh, Freya! How did you ever end up here?"

Untying Alyse's hands, Freya motioned for her to sit down by one of the sets of manacles, then gave her time to massage her rope-burned wrists. "Not by choice, Lady. That's for sure!"

"Then how?"

"After your grandmother expelled Geoff, Palquo, and me, we decided to travel east to your uncle's camp in The Marches and enlist in one of his legions." Freya locked one manacle ring around Alyse's right wrist. "But Palquo wasn't sure your uncle would let us join."

"Why not?" Alyse asked.

"Because your uncle has a reputation for turning away rohans. He thinks they're unreliable and won't give him their full allegiance."

Alyse blinked rapidly in surprise. "Are you kidding me? I've never heard that about him."

"There's probably a lot about the Commander of the Eastern Legions you haven't heard." Freya attached the other ring around Alyse's left wrist. "Anyway, when we were passing through the area here, Malak's brigands captured us." Her lips pressed into a bitter smile. "Malak gave us the choice of joining his band or dying."

"I bet you didn't have much trouble deciding," Kate said dryly.

"None at all," Freya said as she motioned for Kate to turn around so she could untie her hands.

"Why haven't you run away?" Alyse asked.

Freya pointed Kate to a spot near Alyse, then began attaching a set of manacles to her wrists. "Because once you join, you can't leave. Just after we arrived here, someone tried." Freya's voice turned grim. "What they did to her wasn't pretty, and it took a long time for her to die. Afterward, they dumped her body in the woods for the animals to eat, but close enough so we could hear them feeding and fighting over her carcass."

Freya snapped Kate's right manacle into place with sudden force. "What your matriarch did to us, Lady Alyse, was wrong! We fought the best we could. But there were too many raiders. It wasn't our fault that we were the only defenders at the back gate who survived the charm raid. And it wasn't our fault, either, that the Five Sisters haven't finished weaving our personal tapestries."

"Yes, it was wrong," Alyse said. "You all had served my family faithfully."

"Palquo was always a good man," Freya said as she secured the second manacle on Kate's other wrist. "But his expulsion turned him bitter and hateful. He loathes you Dejunes. All he talks about is getting his revenge someday."

"I hope this isn't the day," Kate said, her face expressionless.

"Only the Five Sisters know that." Freya turned to Alyse. "But what are you and Kate doing here so far from home?"

Briefly, Alyse told Freya about her forced marriage to Troy Estati and how she had decided to seek refuge with her uncle. "I'm hoping Uncle Leoc can persuade my grandmother to change her mind about the marriage. Maybe agree to have Mora marry him after all. She certainly wants to."

"That was a dangerous journey you went on," Freya said. "Especially by yourselves."

"We hope our journey doesn't end here," Kate said.

Freya's gaze slid to Kate for a moment, then returned to Alyse. She shook her head, perplexed. "The lives of you noblesse are complicated and unhappy."

Kate blew out a breath. "And yours isn't?"

Alyse gripped Freya's arm with both manacled hands. "Freya, please help us! Don't let our journey end here."

"I'd like to help, Lady," Freya responded, gently disengaging Alyse's fingers. "But this isn't the time. It's better to wait until they decide what to do with you. If they choose to ransom you, there'll be nothing to worry about."

"And if they decide to kill us?" Alyse asked, her heart stretched so tight behind her ribs that she felt pain.

Freya replied without hesitation. "Then I'll help you escape."

"What about Geoff? Can we count on him too?"

Freya scowled. "He and I don't talk about things like that. It's much too dangerous. Here, I trust no one. Not even him." Freya paused, then straightened and pursed her lips. "If I do help you escape, you must promise to take me with you because they'll kill me for helping you."

"Of course you'll come with us," Alyse said. "And I know Uncle Leoc will want you as one of his legionaries too."

Freya sent her a tight smile. "Thank you, Lady."

Freya left, locking the door after her.

Kate rose to her feet, her chains rattling and clanking with her movements. She heaved a long sigh. "Well, this is a fine mess we're in."

"Yes, it is, isn't it." With a clatter of chains, Alyse stood up too. The heavy iron links tugged down on her arms. "We have to get out of here."

"Before the brigands decide what to do to us?" Kate asked.

"If possible. If we can make it into the woods—"

"And leave Freya behind to die?"

"She can come with us."

Alyse took firm hold of the chain linked to the right manacle and tried to wrench it out of the wall. After several futile attempts, she tried the other manacle. Kate yanked at her chains, too, just as unsuccessfully. Finally, they gave up.

"They're in too solid," Alyse said, not bothering to hide her discouragement.

"Yeah."

The cousins sank dejectedly back onto the rough floor.

Alyse leaned against the wall as a wave of despair washed over her. "Trying to escape is useless. We'll just have to pray to the One Goddess that the brigands' greed overcomes Palquo's thirst for revenge."

Kate's brown eyes glowed as if a sudden inspiration had just stuck her. When she spoke, her voice was infused with sudden hope. "What about your Kinesi magic? You can use it to pull out the chains."

"Yes!" Alyse said, catching Kate's hope as if it had jumped from Kate to her. "It only comes to me in a crisis—"

"Which this certainly is."

Expectation swelled Alyse's chest until it was ready to burst. She could do this! Settling herself down, she performed her char exercises, consciously willing herself not to rush through them in her eagerness to perform the magic. When she finished, she slowly rose and gazed at the section of chain attached to the log wall. The magic would work. She focused her attention on the link embedded in the wall and pictured it popping out.

The link remained in place.

No! The magic had to work.

She tried again, but nothing happened. Then tried again. And again. And again. Frustration roiled inside her like water in a storm-swept sea. Overwhelmed by frustration, she grabbed links, put a booted foot against the wall, and pulled and pulled until it felt as if her arm muscles would snap. *Come out, Goddess curse you! Come out!*

Still nothing happened.

Smothered by despair, Alyse plopped onto the floor. "It didn't work," she said, choking out each word as a sob. "Why didn't I listen to Priestess Sybil when she told me I should learn how to control all my magic powers? Now it's too late."

Tears of frustration trickled down Alyse's cheeks.

Kate reached out and just managed to place a hand on Alyse's arm. "Not if your family ransoms us."

"But then we'll have to go back home."

"I think doing that is better than staying here and being killed. Don't you?"

Alyse brushed the tears away with her fingers. "Yes," she said with a resigned sigh.

Time crept by until the sparse light through the windows appeared to be from the late afternoon sun. Alyse twitched when a sudden burst of muffled voices and loud shouts came from the larger cabin. Neither cousin could make out the words being yelled, but the brigands seemed to be having a heated argument. Alyse and Kate traded apprehensive looks.

"It doesn't sound good," Alyse said.

"Yeah."

To keep their spirits up, Alyse and Kate stopped listening and spoke about inconsequential things instead—although fear kept lurking like a menacing shadow in the back of Alyse's mind. Eventually, the faint sunlight in the shed started fading as the sun began its slow descent below the horizon. After a while, footsteps approached the shed, a key rattled in the lock, and Freya entered carrying a couple of bowls.

"Here," she said, handing the dishes to the girls.

Alyse glanced at the contents. Meat stew. The sight and smell of the warm food made her stomach growl hungrily, but she set the bowl aside. From the corner of her eye, she saw Kate put down hers too.

"Have they decided yet?" Alyse asked.

Freya shook her head. "No."

From the sound of things," Kate said, "it appears that there's a difference of opinion among the brigands."

Freya nodded glumly, which made dread bloom in her stomach. "They've broken into two factions."

"Over the amount of the ransom?"

"No." Freya appeared reluctant to say more.

"You don't have to tell us," Kate said. "It's over whether to kill us or pay the ransom money. Some want to kill us, and the others want the money."

Freya still hesitated.

"What does the majority want?" Alyse asked. "Of course they want the money. They'd be fools not to."

"It's not a question of what the majority wants," Freya said. "In a band meeting, the vote has to be unanimous."

Alyse drew in a deep breath before asking the next question. "What are the two choices?"

Freya glanced from Alyse to Kate and back to Alyse. She wet her lips with her tongue, obviously reluctant to answer the question.

Icy fingers of apprehension did a slow walk across Alyse's shoulders.

"I see the choices aren't good," Kate said.

Freya stared into the space between Alyse and Kate. "One of them isn't."

The cold fingers gathered at Alyse's neck and began making their slow way down her spine. "What are the choices?"

"The good one first," Kate said.

Freya's eyes shifted to Kate and then to Alyse. "The good one? We release you after receiving the ransom money."

"And the bad one?" Alyse asked, fearing to hear the answer.

Freya drew in a deep breath, and Alyse found herself holding her own breath too. Finally, Freya expelled the air, but Alyse kept hers deep in her lungs, waiting fearfully to hear the answer. Freya's words came reluctantly.

"We get the ransom . . . and then we . . . kill you both."

Two words burst out of Alyse's mouth along with breath. "Kill us?"

"Why would they vote on doing that?" Kate asked.

Anxiety filled Freya's gray eyes. "Because Palquo hates you. And despite how it might have appeared to you in the big cabin, many band members respect him. Others fear him."

"But I defended him in the matriarch's council," Alyse said.

"You're a Dejune. So is Kate. And that's enough for him."

"If they kill us," Alyse said, "my uncle will send his trackers to run each and every one of them down and kill them. Trackers are allowed to enter Caldonian territory, you know."

Freya's lips twitched into a tight smile. "The argument is that your uncle will do that whichever choice we make."

"Not if you make not sending trackers a condition of the ransom."

"They discussed that too," Freya said, massaging the back of her neck. "And it all came down to this: who can trust the word of a noblesse?"

"Where do you stand on this?" Kate asked.

"I'm for setting you free after we get the money," Freya replied.

Kate started to say something, but Freya rushed on, not giving her a chance. "Palquo is gradually winning my faction over to his side. I don't know how much longer I can hold out myself. Being one of the last to switch to the winning side can be held against you. And it can prove fatal."

"What do you mean?"

"Some of Palquo's faction . . . they take you outside to 'persuade' you to change your mind . . . and you don't come back."

Alyse's chains clattered as Alyse grabbed Freya's wrist. "Don't hold out! Switch sides now. One less voice won't make any difference at this point."

After Freya left, Alyse and Kate forced themselves to eat the stew. To Alyse, the food tasted like straw, but she forced herself to chew and swallow because she had to keep up her strength. Kate did the same. By the time they had finished, the sun had sunk below the horizon, and the shed was in darkness.

Alyse leaned back against the wall and stared into the pitchblack darkness. She had no idea how much time had passed, when shouts exploded from the larger cabin. Gradually the voices petered out, and then erupted into a boisterous cheer.

Alyse's insides quivered. "They've decided."

"Yes." Kate's voice sounded tight when she responded.

More time crawled by as Alyse's nerves twisted like the strings on a lute being too tightly tuned. The strings snapped at the sound of a key turning in the lock of the door. The door opened, and Freya stood at the threshold holding an oil lantern in one hand and balancing two earthenware mugs in the other. Alyse blinked as the sudden intrusion of light blinded her. Freya set the landern on the rough floorboards.

"Here," she said, handing the mugs to the cousins. "I brought you some beer."

"To celebrate or commiserate?" Kate asked.

Freya's lips tightened as she avoided looking at either girl.

The stew in Alyse's stomach threatened to gush up into her throat, and she struggled to keep her voice calm as she spoke. "Just tell us."

Freya's bleak gaze sought hers. "They chose death."

CHAPTER 5

Search

RILL AND TROY SAT opposite each other at the trestle table in the Red Oak Inn. They had ordered breakfast for themselves and were waiting for the others to come down to join them. Troy scowled at Rill. When Troy spoke, he kept his voice low so it wouldn't carry to the people eating breakfast at the nearby tables in the common room. "We'll capture them and make them take us to their camp," he said, his tone seething with sarcasm. "Great plan!"

Rill blew out his cheeks, his reaction a mix of guilt at failing and anger at Troy's unjust accusation. "How was I to know they wouldn't show up last night? I told ya it was a gamble. Weren't ya listening?"

He braced himself for Troy's retort, but the serving girl chose that moment to place bowls of hot porridge topped with berries and clay goblets of watered wine before them. The two teens waited, fighting to keep their pent-up tempers under control in her presence. She read their moods and retreated quickly.

Troy leaned halfway across the table, his blue eyes shooting sparks at Rill. "Because of you, we wasted a whole day here when we could've been searching for Alyse. If anything happens to her because of the delay, I'll hold you personally responsible. So will my uncle."

"You agreed to the plan," Rill said.

"Under duress."

"Duress?" Rill half rose and bent his body toward Troy, closing the gap between them until their faces were only a hand's width apart. The sparks from his blue eyes clashed with Troy's. "I didn't see no duress."

"Why, you damned—"

"Boys, boys," a chiding voice said. "Don't argue in public. It's *so* unseemly, especially for noblesse."

Startled, Rill glanced toward the speaker and found Livia standing beside him. She sent him and Troy a pair of bright smiles. Neither boy was in the mood to return them.

Troy bobbed his head at Rill. "He's not a noblesse."

But I will be. Rill smothered the urge to shout the words at Troy.

Livia sat down beside Rill, who settled back onto the bench. After a moment's hesitation, Troy slowly sank back down, too, while Livia took a sip of wine from Rill's goblet.

Troy pointed at Rill with a sharp flick of his chin. "We lost an entire day because of *him*. And the more time that goes by, the more likely Alyse will be killed. If she hasn't been already."

"What about Kate?" Rill asked. "She might of been killed too. Or ain't ya concerned about her?"

"She's just a backwatcher," Troy responded with a dismissive shrug.

An image flashed through Rill's mind of Kate defending him and Alyse in the One Goddess Temple. Anger clawed at his chest, and he started to get to his feet again. "Why, you son of a—"

Livia grabbed Rill's arm. "Easy there. We have an audience, don't forget."

Rill had forgotten. Casting a look around, he saw women and men at the other tables staring at them—at *him*. He quickly plopped back down. Livia patted his arm approvingly. Her casual show of sisterly affection made Rill feel even closer to her.

"You're the leader, Little Brother," Livia told Troy. "What's our next move?"

Livia's reference to Troy as "Little Brother" gave Rill an odd feeling because he still had trouble believing that he, not Troy, was her actual brother. Once again, he wondered what Troy's reaction would be if he ever learned the truth: that he—Troy—was actually Livia's first cousin and that she and Rill shared the same mother, which made them half sister and half brother.

Troy flung Livia a dirty look in reply.

"You do have a fallback plan," Livia said. "Right?"

Troy's answer came grudgingly. "Not yet."

Livia rolled her blue eyes toward the ceiling rafters. "Don't you think you should come up with one soon? Like before we finish breakfast?"

All three fell silent when the serving girl returned to place Livia's porridge bowl, spoon, and wine goblet in front of her on the trestle table.

"We can track 'em," Rill said when the serving girl left. "That's one reason why Lord Deuth had me come with you. 'Cause I know how to do it."

"Who's tracking what?" Magnus asked, easing himself onto the bench on the other side of Livia.

Before anyone could respond, Yall and Jade took places across from him, on either side of Troy. Magnus caught the serving girl's attention with a wave of his hand, and signaled for her to bring over three more meals.

Troy jabbed a finger at Rill. "That *apprentice* mage caused us a day's delay. Now he wants to track the girls. He thinks he's a hound dog."

Yall sniggered, but Magnus's response cut him off. "Good idea. Rill does know how to track. That's one of the reasons your uncle had him come with us. Remember?"

Troy ground his teeth in irritation.

Magnus's silver-gray eyes fastened on Rill's. "What you told Lord Deuth is the truth, right? You *can* track."

"Been doin' it all my life," Rill said, pride in his tone. Then he told everyone how he and Jedd had tracked a cougar that had killed his horse, to its lair in the mountains. Even as he spoke, his mind's eye saw the charms and staffs in the sarcophagi of the Old Mages he and Jedd had discovered in the den, which was really a huge tomb. He silently renewed his vow to return there after he had become a full-fledged mage to claim them as his own.

Troy's bitter words shattered the images and tugged Rill back to the present. "So instead of tracking them yesterday, we spent the whole bloody time here sitting on our asses."

Livia rapped her spoon on the tabletop. "Boys, boys. Let's not argue over might-have-beens. The question is: should we take Rill's suggestion and track the girls *today*?"

"My answer is yes," Magnus said. "And if we don't have luck tracking them, perhaps the bandits will show up here tonight."

"Thank you, Magnus," Livia said. "That certainly makes sense." She stared pointedly at Troy. "Don't you agree, Little Brother?"

"Yes," Troy replied. "We'll find out if the apprentice mage here can do as he claims or is just a blowhard."

They set out right after breakfast, riding their horses at a slow walk with Rill in the lead, searching for signs on either side of the dirt road. Few travelers were about yet, so they had most of the narrow roadway to themselves. But as the sun rose higher, they found themselves sharing the roadway with riders, tinkers, merchants, and wayfarers, along with an occasional farmer in a cart pulled by a horse or mule. Every so often, Rill dismounted to check tracks by the roadside. Each time Rill climbed back into the saddle, Troy and Yall snickered and made snide remarks about his "so-called" tracking skills. It took all Rill's willpower to ignore them when he really wanted to punch them in their laughing faces.

Toward noon, Troy's impatience with Rill finally exploded. "Can't you hurry up?"

Rill, who was kneeling by the edge of the road, took his eyes off the hoofprints he was examining and hurled Troy a cold look. "Not if ya wanna find Lady Alyse."

"Some tracker," Yall sneered. "It's obvious he doesn't know what he's doing."

Jade sniggered. "Yeah. He's got quite an inflated opinion of his tracking skills. Or he's lying about them."

Livia urged her mare up beside Yall's horse. "Do you want to look for tracks?" she asked, her words slashing at him like the ends of a cat o' nine tails. She turned in her saddle toward Jade, her blue eyes emitting a challenge. "Or do you?"

Neither backwatcher responded.

"Because if either of you thinks you can do a better job than Rill," Livia said, "take over the search and start tracking."

Yall made a jeering sound. "Lady Livia's soft on Rill."

Twisting in his saddle, Troy seized Yall's arm in a tight grip. "Remember your place! That's my sister you're talking to, not some commoner farmgirl."

Anger swept across Yall's face before a deferential mask slid over it. "My apologies, Lord."

"Not to me," Troy said, releasing his hold. "To my sister."

Yall turned his head toward Livia. "Forgive me, Lady. I was out of line."

Livia acknowledged his words with a slight nod.

Rill stood up. "Let's go back."

"Go back?" Troy said.

Jade snorted. "Yall's right after all. Rill can't track. So he's giving up."

Livia made an angry sound in her throat as she maneuvered her mare toward Jade's horse. "I told you to—"

Rill ground his teeth, then stood in his stirrups. "Stop squabbling!"

His unexpected outburst shocked both girls into paralysis. Rill swallowed to give himself time to stomp out his flareup of anger, then spoke in a calm tone. "Actually, I wanna go back and reexamine some places we already looked at. It's been a couple of days since the girls were captured, and there's been a lot of traffic on the road since then. That's made finding signs more difficult."

"But you *can* find them," Livia said pointedly.

Rill appreciated his sister's loyalty, but he had to be truthful. "If they haven't been blotted out by other hoofprints and wheel marks."

"We should've been doing this yesterday," Troy grumbled.

"Well, we didn't, Little Brother," Livia told him. "So let's just accept the current situation and get on with finding the girls."

They returned the way they had come. Rill dismounted several times to examine hoofprints and other traces he might have overlooked the first time around, but they proved to have been made by everyday traffic. Soon he became aware of derisive glares boring into his back like carpenters' drill bits. Troy's, Yall's, and Jade's . . . they believed he would fail. Perhaps they even wanted him to fail. Rill's mind recoiled from the thought of what Lord Deuth's reaction would be if he returned without Alyse. But he feared even more that his failure would smash a ragged hole through Livia's faith in him. His determination to not let down the three most important girls in his life— Livia, Alyse, and Kate—gave him the strength to boot out his fear of failure and keep searching.

Finally, in the early afternoon, Rill came upon a set of tracks alongside a thicket of thorny, impassable bushes surrounded by dense woods. He recalled noticing the jumble of hoof marks in the morning but had thought they'd been made by horses whose riders had paused briefly by the edge of the hard-packed dirt road. Now he wasn't so sure. He dismounted and took a closer look. What he saw made his pulse jump. He stood up with a grin, self-confidence coursing through his veins, like a river gushing after a heavy storm, and faced his companions.

"They went through these bushes," he said, pointing.

Troy looked askance at him. "Through those? You're crazy!"

Troy's caustic remark sent heat gushing through Rill's body. Rill glowered at him. "Yeah. They went through these. And, no, I ain't crazy."

Yall and Jade traded amused smiles.

"He wants so much to succeed," Jade said, "it's embarrassing."

Yall gave a derisive snort. "The poor boy. He doesn't know when to admit defeat."

The urge churned in Rill to yank both of them off their horses and punch them, and it took all his willpower to stay in place.

Troy nodded in agreement. "It's about time he admitted he can't find the girls." Crossing his palms on his saddle horn, he leaned toward Rill. "I don't know about tracking. But I do know that if brigands went through those bushes, their horses would've trampled them. And the bushes look in pretty good condition to me. Besides that, in case you haven't noticed, those are *thorn*bushes. No horse would go through them."

Rill grinned at him, which must have set off Yall.

"We've wasted over half a day, thanks to him," Yall said. "Let's go back to the inn and pray to the One Goddess that an outlaw or two shows up tonight. Then we can—"

Rill lobed Yall a challenging look. "And if none show up? What happens then?"

Yall's lips formed a spiteful smile. "Then we'll go back and tell Lord Deuth his apprentice mage sealed Lady Alyse's fate by his incompetence as a tracker."

"That's right, Lord Troy," Jade said, a malicious light dancing in her hazel eyes as if she were happy with their failure to rescue Alyse and Kate. "Lady

Maude won't be pleased, either. But at least you can rest easy knowing that Lady Mora is more than willing to marry you."

Troy glowered at her, his blue eyes shooting sparks. "It's Lady Alyse I want to marry, *not* Lady Mora."

Troy began to say something else, but Magnus put a hand on Troy's arm and spoke first. "If they went that way," he said to Rill, "how did they get through the thornbushes? They're quite a barrier."

Rill shrugged. "Don't know yet."

"Let's find out," Livia said, scrambling down from her mare. She eased an arm through the thornbushes, then jerked it back. "Ouch!"

Yall, Jade, and even Troy chuckled.

"That's not funny!" Livia said as she sucked her pricked finger.

Hands on hips, Rill studied the thornbushes intently. A section of them didn't look quite natural. He went over to it and gingerly worked his arm through, trying to avoid the thorns. His heart jumped like a fish from water when his hand touched something solid. He ran his fingers along a thick, round piece of vertical wood. It wasn't natural growth but a rail of some sort, shaped by hand. He slowly moved his hand up the rail, and stopped when his fingers hit against something. Something metal. A bar whose ends curved around the rail. He pushed up on the bar.

"A latch!" Rill called over his shoulder as the section of underbrush, now unlatched, move slightly. He gingerly withdrew his arm, ignoring the thorns scraping his hand and tunic sleeve, and rose to his feet. "There's a gate here."

Drawing his sword, Rill gently pushed it through the tangle of thorns until the tip contacted something solid. A horizontal fence rail. He pushed the blade against the wood, and the fence moved slowly inward to reveal a narrow pathway through the shrubbery, wide enough for a single horse and rider to traverse. Parts of thornbushes had been skillfully lashed to the rails so that their roots remained in the ground even as the gate moved inward. The trail itself had been packed down by the hooves of horses that had gone back and forth along it countless times. Obviously, the brigands had used this secret way for a long, long while. A similar camouflaged gate was at the other end of the trail.

Livia glared at Troy. "I suppose you're not even going to apologize to Rill for what you said."

Troy made a face.

Rill anxiously scanned both directions of the road. No one was in sight. "Let's go through and shut the gate behind us before anyone comes along." Without waiting for a response, Rill grabbed his gelding's reins and led it through the opening.

Livia tugged on her mare's reins. "Come on!" she called over her shoulder. "You heard Rill. Get moving before someone happens along the road. And the last one through, be sure to close and latch the gate."

By the time the rest of the searchers reached the other end of the pathway, Rill was already on his knees examining trampled leaves, twigs, and dirt.

"Now what?" Troy asked as Magnus hooked the gate behind them.

"They definitely came this way," Rill replied. "So we'll follow their tracks."

Rill remounted his horse and led the party off at a slow walk following the signs, which took them over hills, through woods, across open fields, and even through a couple of rivers. Twice Rill lost the tracks and had to cast around before finding them again. Finally, they entered a large woods. After a while, Rill became concerned about the whispered chitchat among Troy, Yall, and Jade, even after he asked them to stop, and about the noise their horses were making by stepping on dry leaves and snapping twigs lying on the ground. So he dismounted, exchanged his staff for his longbow and quiver, and went ahead on foot while the others followed some distance behind.

Rill stumbled upon the brigands' camp in the late afternoon.

He was treading quietly through the forest of oak, beech, cedar, pine, and fir trees when a sudden flash of movement from behind a large oak tree up ahead caught his attention. Rill ducked behind a large bush, then peered around the edge. A man, who wore a sword and dagger belted around his waist, walked into view from behind the trunk. He carried a war spear.

A lookout!

The man peered in Rill's direction for a long time, scanning the woods, and then stepped back out of sight behind the tree trunk.

Rill eased an arrow from his quiver, knocked it onto the bowstring, and pulled the bow to half draw. Then, on stealthy feet, he circled around, slipping from tree to bush to tree. Each step he took ratcheted his nerves tauter and tauter because he expected to hear at any moment the noise of his companions' horses bumbling through the forest toward the sentry. He had to take the man down before that happened. As Rill drew nearer to the oak tree, faint sounds of laughter and shouting wafted through the warm afternoon air toward him.

The brigands' camp.

Rill continued creeping closer and closer until the guard, who was leaning on his spear looking bored and peering toward the bandits' hideout, came into view.

Just then, a horse whinnied from Troy's direction.

The sentry stiffened, then started to turn toward the noise.

Rill stepped into view, bow fully drawn. "One sound and you're dead."

The man froze.

Rill ordered the guard to lie facedown and stood over him until the others arrived. After gagging the man, Yall tied his hands behind his back and dragged him deeper into the woods, out of shouting distance of the camp, and sat him down with his back against a tree trunk. Rill untied the gag.

Troy tapped his staff against the man's brown leather boots, then flipped up the bottom of the soiled, once elegant, unbuttoned vest. "Who did you murder for these, I wonder."

The outlaw glared at him.

"Livia, Troy, and Magnus," Rill said. He jerked a thumb at the prisoner. "Can any of you cast a compulsion spell on him to make him tell the truth?"

Livia shook her head. "I'm an illusionist, remember."

"I'm a warrior mage," Jade said.

Magnus nodded. "Same here. But Lord Troy's wearing an Archmage charm."

Troy hesitated as if reluctant to speak. "Yes, I'm wearing one, but . . . well, I've learned mostly Warrior spells. And I haven't learned any Mindbender spells yet."

Yall drew his dagger and sent the brigand a nasty grin. "I can make him talk without casting a spell." He uttered a grim chuckle. "Might be a little painful for him, though."

Yall stepped toward the prisoner.

Fear turned the man's face ashen, and his lips trembled.

Rill blocked Yall's path, placing his back to the outlaw. "Let's wait till we hear his answers." He winked at Yall. "The last time you "questioned" someone, it made me so sick I threw up all over her. And I don't want this one to die before he can give us answers."

Yall made an slight nod, indicating he understood. "I'll try not to get too carried away this time."

"All right," Rill said. "If he doesn't want to talk, or we don't think what he tells us is truthful, you can use your 'compulsion' on him. But I wanna be far out of hearing distance before you start."

"Same here," Livia said, playing along with Rill. "And I have a much harder stomach than Rill. It was disgusting watching poor Rill puke all over the prisoner's corpse."

The lookout proved to be a willing talker, telling them that Alyse and Kate were locked in the shed between the two log houses. Two of the group had left the day before for Caldon to demand a ransom for the girls. And the brigands numbered thirty-eight. Except for the two who had left, all were in camp. He ended by saying that the band included seven mages and that all of them wore Warrior charms.

"Shall I kill him now?" Yall asked Troy, matter-of-factly.

"Sure," Troy replied.

"Please!" the man cried, desperation infusing that single word. He leaned toward them and spoke in a deep and gravelly voice. "I'm just a farmer. They took my matriarch's farm 'cause she couldn't pay a debt, and left my family to starve. Bein' an outlaw is the only way I can make a living to help feed my family." He ended on a plaintive note. "I ain't never killed nobody. Not in cold blood, anyways."

Yall reached for his dagger.

"Wait!" Livia said.

Yall stopped, the blade half out of its scabbard.

Livia stepped closer to the brigand. "Who stole your farm?"

The man's eyes scanned the expensive clothes she and Troy wore and the Estati and Dejune livery on the others. He wet his lips as if he feared answering. "The . . . the noblesse."

"We don't need to hear this crap," Troy said.

Livia motioned for him to be quiet. "Did they actually steal it, or did they buy it?"

"Oh, they paid for it," the man said, his voice laced with bitterness. "But not enough that we could live on." He hawked and spat on the ground. "Not even a mouse could survive on the pittance they gave us."

"Sour grapes," Troy said. He nodded to Yall. "Finish him off."

"No!" Livia turned toward Troy, hands on hips and outrage flushing her face. "You can't just kill him in cold blood."

"Why not?" Troy asked. "He's just a brigand."

"Yes," Jade said. "And that crap about his family . . . it's just a lie to win our sympathy."

Livia's eyes took on a panicked look.

Troy motioned to Yall. "Go ahead."

Gripping the man by his long, unkempt hair, Yall yanked his head back to expose his throat.

Rill glanced at Livia and was overcome by her horrified expression. He clasped Yall's knife wrist in a rock-hard grip. "No!"

"Oh, for One Goddess's sake," Yall said in exasperation. "Will you all please make up your minds. Do you want him dead or alive?"

"Why not?" Troy asked Rill, irritation clipping the words.

Rill said the first excuse that came to mind. "'Cause we might need him later."

Troy frowned and glanced at the others as if seeking their opinions.

"I hate to agree with him," Jade said. "But Rill might be right. If it turns out we don't need him, then we can kill him."

"I agree," Magnus said. "We shouldn't be too hasty. Once dead, we can't bring him back."

Troy pressed his lips together while he considered what they'd said, then nodded. "All right. We'll let him live . . . for now."

The outlaw slumped back against the tree trunk in relief.

Yall retied the gag over the man's mouth and then grinned nastily at him. "A short reprieve."

"I'm going up ahead to take a look," Rill said. "I wanna see the layout of their camp. I also heard a lot of shouting. I wanna see what that was about too."

Troy snatched up his staff, which he'd propped against a tree. "I'm going with you."

"Me too," Yall said.

"Same here," Jade said.

Rill lifted his chin in a challenge. "Ain't none of ya comin' with me."

Troy's eyes narrowed. "Why not?"

"'Cause you all sound like a bunch of oxen trampling on timber. That's a sure way to let the brigands know we're here."

Jade stepped toward Rill, closing the distance between them until they were almost face-to-face. "I answer to the Dejunes. No Estati apprentice tells me what to do."

"Then I will," Troy said, his blue eyes lobbing fireballs at Jade. "Your matriarch put you under my family's authority. Right here and now, that means my authority. Rill goes, and the rest of us stay, including you. If you don't like that, you can return to Caldon and tell Lady Maude why I sent you back."

"And you'd better not do anything to put Alyse's or Kate's lives at risk," Livia added. "I know you're Mora's girl, and I'll be keeping an eye on you."

Troy motioned for Rill to be off.

Rill slipped quietly past the trees and bushes to where he'd captured the lookout. As he approached the spot, he began hearing the brigands' voices from their hideout somewhere beyond the trees. The sounds grew louder with each step forward. When he neared the edge of the woods, Rill dropped onto his stomach and crawled over dead branches and twigs and dry leaves to the edge of the tree line. He found himself looking down a gentle, grassy slope onto an equally grassy clearing. He didn't consider the site a good location for their hideout because attackers could surround their camp and bottle them in.

Two log cabins with porches of roughly split lumber, which were probably the outlaws' living quarters, stood a short distance beyond the midpoint of the clearing. Bandits sat in chairs on the porches of both dwellings and on the porches' steps watching some of their comrades playing a rough game of shoveball, and cheering them on. Several women and men were sharpening knives, swords, and spearheads instead of watching the game. A log shed squatted between the shacks. Two long, high wood stacks—one of cut timber for firewood and the other of uncut logs—rose opposite each other a short distance in front of the shack, separated by a wide, clear space. A chopping block surrounded by wood chips was just inside the opening. Rill pictured himself and his companions crouching between the two log piles. A short distance away stood a rickety barn with an attached corral in which several horses were munching grass.

In the extreme rear, behind the shed, was what appeared to be a two-seater outhouse made of poorly split logs. A brigand, who appeared to be a man with dark-brown hair, was leaning with his back against the space between the two doors, arms folded, waiting his turn. The right-hand door opened, and the outlaw unfolded his arms and turned toward it. Rill drew in a surprised breath when he saw a brown ponytail swing with the motion and noticed breasts in the bandit's profile. The brigand was a woman. Then someone stepped through the outhouse door. Rill gasped, sending his breath rushing down his throat.

Alyse!

The woman escorted Alyse to the shed, unlocked the door, and accompanied her inside. A short time later, the woman emerged, relocked the door, and went inside the larger cabin.

Rill studied the clearing and the outlaws playing on the grassy field and sitting on the porches. His group was too small, even with three warrior mages—plus Troy's Warrior spells—to rescue Alyse and Kate from a band that size by force. He and the others had to use stealth instead.

Rill's gaze shifted back to the porch of the larger cabin.

A man who had been sharpening a spearhead lay the weapon aside. Climbing to his feet, he entered the building and came back out a short time later strapping a sword and dagger around his waist. He said something to his compatriots that made them laugh. Then, picking up the spear, he went down the steps and started across the clearing.

Rill's breath caught in his throat.

The lookouts were changing shifts!

CHAPTER 6

Livia Shines

HIS HEART RACING LIKE a horse at full gallop, Rill elbowed himself backward from the tree line, then leaped to his feet, and sprinted into the woods where the others were waiting with the prisoner.

"They're changing lookouts!" he said. "The new one's on his way here."

Troy cursed, his fear palpable. "What're we going to do? He'll sound the alarm when he discovers the sentry's missing."

"We take him prisoner," Jade said.

Frowning, Magnus fingered his chin through his gray beard. "There's a problem with that."

"Which is?" Jade asked.

"When he doesn't return," Magnus replied, nodding at the prisoner, "they'll suspect something's wrong."

Frenzied anxiety swept across Yall's face. "Thirty-four against six! "We don't stand a chance against those odds."

"Against *five*," Troy said. "My sister can't fight."

Livia made a *harrumph* sound. "I can too!"

The others ignored her as they traded apprehensive glances.

"Not even Lady Maude would condemn us for pulling out," Jade said, a tremor of fear in her tone. She looked directly at Troy. "Do you agree?"

Troy stood mute, gnawing on the inside of his cheek.

"Do you *agree*, Lord Troy?" Jade asked again, her tone now urgent.

Troy swallowed several times, then straightened his shoulders. "You're right. Let's get going."

Rill's mind spun from this unexpected turn of events. But he stepped into Troy's path when Troy headed toward the horses. "You ain't serious. We can't abandon the girls now that we've found 'em."

"Stay if you want," Troy told him and brushed on by.

Livia seized Troy's arm and yanked him around so violently that he almost lost his balance. Putting her hands on her hips, she faced into him, almost nose to nose. "Maybe I can't fight. But I'm an illusionist." She stomped over to the prisoner, touched the orb of her staff to his flesh, and muttered a spell. Immediately, her body shimmered . . . and slowly morphed into the lookout's.

Rill's eyes matched the prisoner's as they widened in wonderment.

Livia glowered at everyone, her free hand on her hip in a very un-Livia-like manner, and spoke in the sentry's deep, gravelly voice. "Well, ain't any of you scum comin' with me? We gotta capture the replacement."

Rill grinned, relieved by her unqualified support and amused by her transformation. "I'll go."

"Me too," Yall said with a grin.

Rill loosened his sword in its scabbard. "The rest of ya stay here with the prisoner."

After Livia exchanged her staff for the prisoner's spear, she, Rill, and Yall headed for the tree where the sentry had been posted. Just before reaching it, they hung back, letting Livia go the rest of the way alone. She settled into position moments before the replacement arrived.

"Anything to report?" the man asked.

"Naw," Livia replied, shaking her head. "Same ole, same ole." As she spoke, she shifted her position, making the man move with her, until his back was to Rill and Yall. "What about them girlies? What's doin' with 'em?"

"Nothin'," the man said. "But we gotta keep our hands off 'em, though . . . for now, anyways." The brigand sniggered. "Waste of good girl flesh, if ya ask me."

Rill nodded to Yall. He'd expected that they would move together, but Yall went more quickly.

"No one asked you," Yall said as he reached the man.

Before the brigand could react, Yall slung an arm around his neck and plunged his dagger into his back. The man jerked, then went limp. Yall eased the body onto the ground.

Livia gaped at the corpse, white-faced.

Anger flared in Rill, and he struck Yall on the shoulder. "What did ya kill him for?"

Nonchalantly, Yall wiped the bloody knife blade on the dead man's pant leg. "Seemed like a good idea."

"I wanted him alive."

Yall shrugged. "You should have told me."

Rill hurled him a withering look. "We can't just leave him here. Help me move him to someplace where he won't be found."

He and Yall lugged the corpse deeper into the woods and concealed it behind some bushes. Then the three of them returned to where the others were waiting anxiously.

As soon as Jade spotted Livia, her eyes widened until her whites surrounded her brown iris. "What're you doing here?"

"What d'ya mean?" Livia asked.

"You were *relieved*."

"Yeah. So what?"

"So you're expected in *their* camp, not ours."

Livia stood motionless as if Jade's words had turned her into a statue. "What do I do now?"

"You go down to their camp and blend in," Jade said.

Livia gulped down a nervous swallow.

"Jade's right," Rill said, putting a comforting hand on Livia's shoulder. "You'll be our spy. Find out whatever information you can that'll help us free the girls. Then come back." He paused and smiled encouragingly at her. "Don't worry. Everything will be fine."

"Everything will be fine!" Livia rattled off a string of colorful curses. Everyone gawked at her in amazement. She put a hand to her mouth, equally surprised. "Sorry," she said in a rough tone. "When I touched the friggin' bastard . . . er, brigand, with my staff, I absorbed a bit of his essence. So I can't always control the words I use. They're his, not mine. It's part of the illusion."

"Which means you'll be fine," Rill said, squeezing her shoulder encouragingly. "Just like I said."

Livia rocked in place for a moment. "But . . . but what if I slip up?"

The brigands would kill her, Rill knew. But he refused to tell her that. He fished around in his mind for a less scary answer.

"Trust your illusion," Troy told her. "The impulses it gives you belong to the man you're impersonating." He grinned at her. "As you've already shown us."

Livia closed her eyes and took a deep breath. Then she opened her eyes and smiled at him. "You're right, Little Brother."

"You'd best be going," Troy said softly. "Before they start wondering where you are."

Livia hugged Troy, clinging tightly to him for a long moment before pulling away. Then they stared at each other. Livia seemed reluctant to move. She bit her lip.

Troy put a hand tenderly to her cheek. "You can do this, Big Sister. I know you can."

Pulling away, Livia set her face resolutely. "I'll do my best."

After she left, Troy turned to Rill, blue eyes narrowed. "If anything happens to her . . ."

Rill's heart shuddered because he had concerns about Livia's safety, too, but he forced himself to appear confident. "She'll be fine. You can trust me on that."

"And if she's not 'fine,'" Troy said, holding Rill's gaze, "you'll be dead. You can trust *me* on that."

Rill suppressed a shudder. But regardless of the threat, he'd risk his life to protect his newfound sister.

Leaving Yall to guard the prisoner, Rill and the others crept up to the timberline and watched Livia cross the meadow to the brigands' camp. A woman near one of the cabins hailed her, and the two of them chatted briefly together. Afterward, Livia circulated among the other bandits who were outside and then entered each cabin for a short time. Before long, Rill's apprehension for Livia's safety slackened.

"Looks like her illusion's working," he said as he observed her lounging on the porch of the larger cabin.

Later, though, as the late afternoon sun crawled toward evening, Rill's anxiety began mounting because Livia had remained longer with the outlaws than he had anticipated. The others were equally worried.

Just as the sun began its descent below the horizon in a blaze of vivid oranges and blood reds, the brigands were called into the larger lodge for supper. They went in eagerly. Most remained inside, but a few came back out carrying tin plates and clay mugs and sat down on the porch chairs and steps to eat.

Instead of going inside to fetch her supper, though, Livia went to the out-house. Moving from one door to another, she knocked on each one, opening it afterward and peering inside. Then she sauntered to the back of the shed where Alyse and Kate were being held.

"What's she up to?" Troy muttered, more to himself than to the others.

"Making contact with Alyse," Rill replied, not taking his eyes from Livia. "How else will Alyse and Kate know we're here?"

A short while later, a brigand emerged from the larger cabin carrying two plates of food and a pair of mugs, which she took to the shed. Squinting hard in the deepening sunset, Rill made out the outlaw's ponytail. The girls' jailer. Setting down the plates and mugs, she unlocked the door and disappeared inside with the food.

"I think that's Freya," Jade said.

"Who?" Rill asked.

Jade quickly explained how Freya, a young protector, and two other Dejune protectors had been expelled by Lady Maude a few months ago for failing to uphold their oaths during a charm raid. "If she's down there," Jade concluded, "I bet Geoff and Palquo are too. I wonder how they ended up here, of all places."

After what seemed like a long time, Freya came out, locked the door, and left with the dirty dishes. A little later, Livia ambled into view from behind the shed and joined the brigands.

By now the outlaws had finished supper, and the shadows were deepening as night set in. Oil lamps were lit on the two porches, and the bandits lounged around in the wavering lamplight. Someone lugged out a keg that had a spigot. Raising a ragged cheer, the brigands crowded around the keg and filled up their mugs. Several women and men pulled out fiddles, pipes, and a mandolin and began playing popular tunes while others, waving their mugs, sang the lyrics with ragged gusto.

Jade peered at a man who was sitting in a chair on the porch of the larger building, swing his mug in time to the music. A nearby lantern threw light onto his murky figure, highlighting a beard and mustache.

"I think that's Palquo," Jade said. "And look over there." She pointed to a man standing near Palquo. "I'm pretty sure that's Geoff."

Rill turned his head toward Jade. "Are they good fighters?"

"Yes."

Her response made Rill's chest tingle. He wished he hadn't asked.

"This might be a long evening," Jade said. "So I'll go back and relieve Yall. He can take my place here."

Magnus pushed himself backward by his elbows. "I'm going too. You should come as well, Rill. Troy can stay. One lookout is enough for now. Besides, as Jade said, this could be a long night, and we'll need to work in shifts."

Still lying on his stomach, Rill shook his head. "I ain't gonna abandon Lady Livia."

"You're not abandoning her," Magnus said. "It's just that she could be down there for a long—"

"Something weird's going on," Troy said.

Rill's gaze snapped to the brigands while Jade and Magnus elbowed their way back to him.

"Livia just went into the outhouse," Troy said. "Left-hand door."

"Perhaps she's taking a dump," Jade said with a trace of sarcasm.

"Then it's odd that Freya has to take one too," Troy responded testily.

Rill peered more closely through the rapidly darkening light. Sure enough. A shadowy figure was making its way to the latrine. "How do you know it's Freya? You can't see no ponytail in this light."

"Because I watched her come through the door onto the porch," Troy said. "The lantern light lit up her features."

What Freya did next puzzled Rill. She knocked on the left-hand door. Livia opened it, brushed by Freya, and headed into the woods behind the privy. Without glancing at Livia, Freya entered the outhouse and closed the door.

Rill traded puzzled looks with his equally bewildered companions. "What was that all about?"

"Livia's on her way back," Troy said, relief obvious in his tone. "So we'll find out from her."

Leaving Jade to watch, Rill and the others returned to camp and waited impatiently for Livia to arrive in her roundabout way through the woods.

"Thank the One Goddess you're back," Troy said when she finally returned.

Livia moved to embrace him but backed off when he flinched. "Oh, sorry," she said. "I forgot." Fetching her staff, she canceled the Illusion spell and morphed back into her real self. She let out a deep breath. "Being cooped up in that body was horrible." She flung a sharp look at the prisoner. "Honestly, I don't know how you can stand yourself."

Rill beckoned everyone to come out of earshot of the brigand, then turned to Livia. "What did ya find out?"

"I did more than find out." Livia reached into her belt purse and pulled out two small objects and held them up.

Rill squinted at them in the darkness. "What are they?"

"Keys. One for the shed door and the other for the girls' shackles." Livia puffed her chest out, obviously pleased with herself.

Rill grinned at his newfound sister in the fading light while pride swelled his heart until it seemed to press against his rib cage. She had gumption.

Everyone else gaped at her, dumbfounded.

"How did you get those?" Troy finally asked.

"From the jailer. A girl named Freya." Livia chuckled as she closed her fingers around the keys. "Did you see me go behind the shed at suppertime?"

"Yes."

"I let Alyse and Kate know we were here. Alyse told me about Freya. She used to—"

"We know about her," Troy said. "Jade told us."

"Well," Livia continued, the sound of that one word showing she was a bit miffed by the interruption, "what you don't know is that Freya wants to get away from here. She's already agreed to help Alyse and Kate escape if she can go with them to The Marches." Livia hesitated, and Rill could hear her swallow saliva. "The brigands plan on killing Alyse and Kate whether or not they get the ransom money."

"We need to get them out now," Troy said.

"How?" Magnus asked. "Even counting Freya, the odds against us are overwhelming."

"We have the keys," Livia said.

Magnus made a dismissive sound. "Having them makes no difference. We'd be committing suicide by—"

"Stealth," Rill said. "We gotta use stealth."

"That's what I thought too," Livia said. "So I told Freya and the girls that we'd make our move at first light tomorrow morning." She grinned at Rill. "Stealthily."

"How?" Rill asked, intrigued.

"By sneaking up to the shed before the outlaws wake up, and setting them free."

"Good plan, Sis," Troy said. "We'll do it. But with one minor change. We'll make our move tonight, as soon as the brigands go to sleep." He held out his hands. "Give me the keys."

Livia was silent for a moment, her indistinct shape rigid, and Rill sensed that she was staring hard at Troy. "I don't think you heard me, Little Brother. I said I told Freya we'd make our move at first light."

"I heard you," Troy said. "But doing it now is better."

"Troy, it's nighttime. Or haven't you noticed."

"Nighttime's no problem. Rill's a tracker. He guided us here. So he can guide us back out too."

Rill mentally rolled his eyes at Troy's näiveté. "Getting out at night ain't as easy as coming in at daytime 'cause I won't be able to see no signs. And what if the bandits hear us bumbling through the woods trying to find a way out? The whole camp would be stirred up like a nest of yellow jackets. We wouldn't stand a chance of making off in the dark." He stepped closer to Troy. "I don't know these woods, but the brigands do."

"We've already got the keys," Troy said in a tone as if he were speaking to a simpleton. "And I'm in charge. I say we're freeing the girls tonight."

Livia folded her hands across her chest and leaned toward Troy. "Who's going to tell Freya about the change in plans? She's leaving with us, remember?"

"Freya's an outlaw." Troy extended his hand toward his sister. "The keys."

Livia put the hand clasping the keys behind her back. "Alyse made an agreement with Freya, and I reconfirmed it. We're *not* leaving without her."

For a long moment, Troy's body went still as a marble statue. Then his brows furrowed, and he said, "I've never seen you so squeamish before about breaking your word. And to a damned bandit, no less."

Livia lifted her chin up, her blue eyes flaring in defiance, which made Rill want to hug her.

"Yeah?" she said. "Well, maybe I'm changing my ways. Anyhow, I have the keys. So what I say goes: we're *not* leaving without Freya."

"You won't have those keys for long," Troy said, stepping toward Livia.

Rill didn't know who Freya was, but if it was important to Livia—as well as to Alyse and Kate—that she come with them, then she would. He placed himself in front of Troy. "The keys stay with Livia."

Troy jeered at him. "And who's going to stop me . . . you?"

Rill stared at Troy's shadowy shape in the darkness, his hand moving toward his sword. "Yeah. Me."

"No, not Rill," Livia said. "Me." Stepping backward deeper among the trees and shrubs, she pulled back her arm for a throw. "If you try to take them from me, Troy, I swear by the One Goddess, I'll fling these keys so far you'll never be able to find them in the dark."

"You wouldn't dare!" Troy said, and Rill could make out the angry creases in his furrowed brow. "That would condemn Alyse to staying here. Great-Grandmother Ariella would expel you if she ever found out"

Livia leaned toward Troy. "And who would tell her—you?"

"We will," Yall said.

Troy spun around to face him. "Butt out of this, all of you!" His shadowy head made an arc that encompassed the others, and Rill pictured Troy's angry eyes burning across their faces. "This is between me and my sister." Breathing hard, Troy turned back to Livia.

Rill still kept himself between the two of them.

"Step away, Rill," Livia said calmly, her arm still poised for a throw. "My brother has an important decision to make."

Rill hesitated, his mind rebelling against her command.

Livia spoke again, her words firm. "Rill, step aside."

Rill took several unwilling steps away.

Troy's breath came in audible blasts as he confronted Livia, one hand gripping his staff and the other forming a fist at his side. Rill's own heart thumped rapidly, and he braced himself to lunge quickly at Troy if he should threaten Livia.

But after a long pause, Troy's shoulders sank and he let out a huge sigh. Then he turned to Yall, Magnus, and Jade. "No one's going to tell anyone about this. Understood?"

Their murky heads bobbed in agreement.

Troy put a hand on Livia's shoulder. "We'll do things your way."

Livia covered his hand with hers. "Good. We'll go in at first light."

CHAPTER 7

Rescue

EARLY THE NEXT MORNING, as the first rays of dawn filtered through the trees in a palette of yellows and oranges, Rill picked up the cloak he'd slept on. Birds chirped happily, fluttering from branch to branch, and the warm early morning air gave promise of a hotter day to come. Scratching under his arm, Rill glanced at his companions who were just stirring.

Late last night, he, Livia, and Magnus had waylaid the lookout who had come to relieve the one Yall had killed. They'd tied her up and put her with the other captive but on the opposite side of the tree. Then Magnus had cast a Paralyze spell on both of them. Everyone assumed—or hoped—the brigands in the camp were fast asleep and wouldn't notice that the sentry who had been relieved had never returned.

Rill glanced toward the captives, and a sudden coldness expanded his chest. He poked Troy's leg with his boot. "Get up! Get up! The prisoners are gone!"

It took a few moments for Rill's words to penetrate his companions' sleepy minds. Then they scrambled to their feet.

"A Paralyze spell doesn't wear off. You need to cast the Mobility spell." Troy rattled the words off quickly. He whirled toward Magnus. "Did you—"

"Cancel them? No. But someone must have." Magnus paused, his silvery eyes blinking rapidly. "Another brigand—a mage—must've come here and canceled the spells."

"Then why are we still alive?" Livia asked. "They could've killed us in our sleep."

"It takes a while to recover from a Paralyze spell," Magnus responded. "Perhaps whoever canceled the spells helped the prisoners back to their camp—"

"And warned the others," Jade said, anxiety filling her hazel eyes.

An image burst into Rill's mind. Yall's bloody corpse by the tree line. He'd been on guard duty. Rill scooped up his sword and buckled it on. "Whoever freed them must of killed Yall. How else could she of gotten by him to get here? She must've warned the other brigands by now, and they—"

"Might be on their way here to attack us," Troy said, a fearful tremor in his voice while he eyed the woods in front of them as if expecting the outlaws to attack at any moment.

Livia gasped in horror. "Alyse and Kate! We won't be able to rescue them."

"If we stay here any longer," Jade said, "we won't be able to rescue ourselves."

Rill struggled to conquer his own panic. They shouldn't react without knowing the lay of the land. "The brigands ain't attacked us yet. Why's that? And what're they doin' now?" He headed for the timberline, his heart racing as fast as his feet.

Livia snatched up her staff. "I'm going with you."

"Me too," Magnus said.

Jade started off with them, but Troy called her back. "Help me saddle the horses. We might need to make a hasty retreat."

Rill sprinted through the woods, Livia and Magnus close on his tail. Suddenly he stopped short, almost stumbling, and blinked in astonishment at a figure ambling toward them.

Yall!

Relief pricked Rill's fear, deflating it. "You all right?"

"Of course." Yall wrinkled his forehead in puzzlement. "Why wouldn't I be?"

"Because the prisoners escaped," Rill said. "That's why. We thought they might of killed you—"

"And the other brigands . . . might be on their way here . . . to kill us," Livia said as she strove to catch her breath.

"Oh, that," Yall said, his tone dismissive. "I was going to tell you."

Rill's eyes narrowed at him. "Tell us what?"

"That I killed them."

Livia's head drew back quickly as if someone had slapped her. "You *what?*"

"Last night before I went on watch. And I stowed their bodies with the other one." Yall wrinkled his nose. "I'll tell you . . . it was a real pain lugging a couple of corpses that have been stiffened with Paralyze spells."

Livia stepped back from Yall as if she feared his closeness might contaminate her. "You *killed* them?"

Yall nodded.

"But we agreed not to."

"I thought it best that we eliminate any possible complications."

Livia drilled Yall with a fierce glare. "That wasn't your decision to make. You're a retainer. We tell *you* what to do, not the other way around."

Yall brushed her words aside with a wave of his hand. "I'm sure Lord Deuth will agree with what I did."

The veins on Livia's neck throbbed as she began to make a retort, but Magnus interrupted in that reasonable-sounding voice he used so often, which sometimes drove Rill mad. "With all due respect, Lady Livia, I think Yall did the right thing. If we'd let the two brigands live, there would've been be two more swords to use against us."

Livia turned her fiery gaze on him. "They were paralyzed, Magnus."

"That's the point," Magnus said. "Killing them was the humane thing to do. After all, would you want to leave them paralyzed? If none of the brigands discovered them after we left, the two sentries would starve to death. Or they'd end up being a meal for the wolves and coyotes. They'd be eaten alive, while their minds and senses were active even though their bodies were paralyzed. What kind of a death is that?"

Livia gave Magnus an anguished stare. "That poor man was trying to feed his family."

"No." Magnus leaned toward Livia. "That poor man was an outlaw, meaning he was outside of the law."

Livia blinked, tears watering her eyes.

Magnus sighed and placed a hand on her shoulder. "Life can be harsh sometimes. And sometimes we must make difficult decisions. Ones that go against our grain."

Livia's lips flattened, and she yanked her shoulder from his grip. "I'm sure Yall's decision didn't go against *your* grain."

Her insult rolled off Magnus, like a marble down an incline. "What's done is done, Lady. If you still think Yall did the wrong thing when we get home, see Lady Ariella. I'm sure she will stand by him, though." Magnus's gaze sought out Rill. "What do *you* think?"

Rill felt as if Magnus had just set a trap for him by forcing him to take sides against Livia. "I . . . well, they *were* brigands. And they would of been executed if they'd been arrested. So I guess Yall did what the law would of done. But he shouldn't of made the decision on his own. It was Lord Troy's to make."

Magnus belted out a hearty laugh. "I've just seen a new side of you, Rill. You're quite the diplomat."

The horses were saddled and waiting by the time Rill returned to camp with the others. After wolfing down a hasty breakfast of journey cakes and water, everyone walked toward the timberline, leading their horses by their reins. Rill went first, fear gnawing at his gut like a hungry wolf, with each step he took. This was nothing like hunting cougars. Glancing over his shoulder at his companions, he wondered if they were frightened too. The whiteness of Livia's tight-lipped face showed she was. And Rill could tell that Troy was striving to mask his own nervousness. But Yall, Magnus, and Jade displayed no outward signs as if to them this were just the beginning of another ordinary workday. Rill envied their composure.

Rill stopped a short distance from the timberline and had everyone tie their horses' reins to sturdy branches. After double-checking the bindings that lashed his staff to his saddle, he crept to the edge of the woods, bow in hand and quiver strapped to his back. The rest of the party followed as quietly as they could.

The brightening sun, which had begun its slow ascent above the trees on the other side of the meadow, was now turning the yellows and oranges into red, making it appear as if the sky were on fire. In the camp, no one was stirring.

Rill felt a flush of relief, and then took several deep breaths to settle his jittery nerves. He pulled a barbed arrow from his quiver and knocked it onto his bowstring. Then he rose into a low crouch.

The others imitated him.

"Come on," Rill said.

He led them down the incline and across the clearing at a run. When they were almost at the prisoners' shed, a figure stepped out from behind the larger cabin. Everyone stopped short. Rill cursed under his breath at their stroke of bad luck and brought up his longbow, aiming the arrow at the brigand while pulling the bow to full draw.

The brigand caught sight of them, stopped short, and waved her hands frantically.

"No!" Livia hissed, clamping her hand on Rill's arm. "It's Freya."

Rill lowered the longbow.

Livia pointed at Freya, then at the shed. Freya shook her head, tapped her chest with a forefinger, and pointed at the stable.

Livia turned to her companion. "She going to saddle horses for the girls."

"Let's go!" Rill said, and started racing toward the camp again.

Everyone chased at his heels.

When they neared the shed, Livia angled off toward it to free Alyse and Kate. Following their plan, Rill turned into the space between the piles of split timber and uncut logs and crouched down just inside the far opening. Jade, Magnus, and Yall took up positions along the length of the passageway and dropped to their knees. Troy knelt just inside the rear opening. Rill watched Livia unlock the shed door and vanish inside, leaving the door ajar. He resisted the urge to go and shut it. Instead, he let out a shaky breath of relief. The first part of the rescue was accomplished. But two more parts still remained: releasing the girls and obtaining horses for them. Rill hoped that wouldn't take long.

He glanced behind him at his companions and saw Jade half stand to look over the top of the split logs at the cabins. "Jade, get down!" he whispered.

Jade scooched back down.

"Keep your heads down, everyone," Troy said softly. "Rill and I are the only ones who'll do the looking."

For Rill, waiting was the hardest part. It seemed as if time were just inching by while the sun cleared the treetops and bathed the clearing in its bright light. Neither Troy's, Magnus's, nor Yall's charms contained a Concealment spell. Rill wished it were still nighttime because the darkness would mask their movements. He kept flicking his eyes back and forth from cabin to shed to cabin and back again. His nerves twisted tighter and tighter. Using the woodpiles wasn't a good idea, he knew, because they had boxed themselves in, allowing the brigands to attack from both ends if they were discovered. A dangerous place to hide but the only one available. His uneasy gaze flicked back to the shed. Livia was taking forever to release the girls.

The squeaking of a door opening and booted feet on wooden planks made Rill's eyes dart to the smaller cabin. A man, armed with a sword and spear, had emerged and was going down the steps. The outlaw stopped several paces from the cabin, presenting his profile to Rill. The man yawned, rolled his shoulders, and stretched his neck to get the kinks out. Then he started strolling across the clearing. Rill cursed under his breath as he grasped the man's intent.

He was relieving the watch!

In one fluid motion, Rill stood, drew back his longbow, and let fly the barbed arrow. The man fell without a sound. Dropping his bow, Rill raced to the body, gripped it under the arms, and started dragging it across the grass toward the stacks of firewood to hide it from sight. He cast a glance over his shoulder and mumbled a curse.

The door of the larger cabin opened. A woman stepped onto the porch. Her body turned rigid with shock when she spotted him.

Shod hooves clattered on floorboards inside the stable, and Freya rode out on horseback, leading two other horses by their reins. At the same time, the shed door flew open, and Livia, Alyse, and Kate rushed out.

"To arms!" the woman hollered. "We're under attack! The prisoners are escaping!"

Rill released the body and gripped his sword's handle.

"To arms, everyone! We're under—" A dagger flung from the stacks of wood buried itself in the woman's chest.

Rill sprinted toward the woodpiles to fetch his longbow while Yall ran toward the woman to retrieve his dagger.

The commotion spooked the three horses. Freya's jumped sideways. Freya released the other horses' reins and struggled to control her mare.

Kate retrieved the weapons from the woman Yall had killed while Yall stood beside her, sword drawn.

Jade and Magnus joined them.

The four of them watched the cabin, ready to fight.

Rill stood in the space between the two wood stacks as he nocked another arrow on his bowstring. He muttered a string of silent curses that would make the One Goddess blush while his heart pounded so rapidly that his chest ached. Just their luck that their plan fell to pieces at this crucial moment. But there was nothing he could do about it now, but fight.

Livia and Alyse joined them.

"I've never been happier in my life to see you," Alyse said to Rill. She nodded at Troy. "Both of you."

"Yeah?" Rill's expectant gaze hopped back and forth from cabin to cabin, waiting for the reaction to the woman's shout. "Well, save your thanks till we're outta here."

Freya, her mare finally under control, rode up to them and dismounted. She handed the reins to Alyse.

Rill pointed across the clearing, his quick-spoken words reflecting his urgency. "Ride up there. Horses are tethered inside the tree line. We'll join ya once you're out of danger."

"We'll all go together," Alyse said.

"Just do as I say, damn it!" Rill snapped. "And do it *now*."

Alyse flinched as if he had physically slapped her, then swung into the saddle like a practiced horsewoman. She extended a hand to Livia. "Get up behind me."

Livia hesitated. "I'm here to rescue you."

Just then, the doors of two cabins slammed open. Brigands—some of them half dressed and all of them armed with swords, spears, and axes—spilled out like two swarms of bees.

"There they are!" a woman shouted, pointing at Kate and her fellow backwatchers.

"Look, there's more!" another brigand hollered. "By the woodpiles. Let's get 'em!"

"I want those bastards taken alive!" a rage-filled voice—Palquo's—hollered. "All of them!"

Some outlaws ran for the woodpiles while others charged toward Kate, Magnus, Yall, and Jade.

Troy aimed an exasperated growl at Livia. "She's just been rescued. So get up there!"

Troy boosted Livia up behind Alyse.

Alyse pressed her heels against her horse's flanks, and the mare took off across the meadow toward the woods.

Brigands split off from the two groups and raced after the mare.

Standing by the embedded ax, Rill shot an arrow at the lead brigand chasing the girls. From the corner of his eye, he noticed a group of outlaws had almost reached the woodpiles. He pivoted, releasing three swift arrows.

A mage cast a spell at them, but Troy countered it.

And then the brigands were too close for spell casting or arrows.

Rill backed into the space between the piles, dropping his longbow and drawing his sword with one hand and his dagger with the other.

Troy's shout sounded behind him. "Here they come, Freya!"

Yells and the clanging of steel on steel rose from beyond the charging brigands as Kate, Yall, Jade, and Magnus desperately fought a huge pack of bandits.

Rill didn't hold out much hope for them, or for Troy, Freya, and himself. But an unexpected peace settled over him. As long as Alyse and Livia made it to safety, his death would be a small price to pay for keeping them alive.

And then Rill's inner peace shattered when the outlaws arrived and surrounded the woodpiles.

A woman thrust a spear at him.

Rill banged it away with the flat of his blade, then thrust his sword into her belly.

Another brigand pressed in, stepping on the dead woman's chest.

Rill cut him down too.

An angry voice rose above the shouts and clangs of steel on steel. "Alive! I want them all alive!"

The remaining bandits backed away from the entrance. Some disappeared, but many stood at either opening, weapons in hand, making it impossible for Rill, Troy, and Freya to escape.

Rill exchanged puzzled looks with Troy and Freya.

Suddenly wood from the split kindling pile toppled into the passageway. Rill jumped backward, mumbling a profanity. The brigands were shoving the kindling into the opening between the two piles. This was something Rill hadn't anticipated. He traded anxious looks with Troy and Freya. "We gotta get outta here!"

More split logs landed between Troy and Freya. Troy slashed at an exposed arm. The blade cut all the way through. The victim screamed, "We're hemmed in."

More and more firewood came tumbling down while Rill slashed at exposed hands and arms that were shoving the kindling.

"Push from the middle!" a voice cried. "We'll bury 'em under the wood."

"Idiot!" another voice shouted. "Didn't ya hear Palquo say he wants 'em alive? Push from the top and flush 'em out."

Rill stepped back as several pieces of firewood fell on the spot he'd been occupying. He traded desperate looks with Troy and Freya. "We gotta make a run for it!"

Troy stepped back from a hail of kindling, almost tripping on wood scattered behind him. "How? We're trapped in here."

"We ain't got no choice."

"Running is suicide."

"So is stayin'."

Just then a voice said, "Are you sure he said we can do it?"

"Yeah," another voice responded. "Palquo said he doesn't care now if they're half dead. He'll still get his revenge."

Hoots and hollers followed the words.

"Now," the voice yelled, "all together . . . heave!"

Horror overwhelmed Rill. It was too late to run. And he was going to die.

Wood all along the pile began toppling over.

\#

Alyse dug her heels into the mare's flanks, urging the horse on. Livia wrapped her arms tightly around Alyse's chest, her staff clutched in both hands. A red streak shot past the horse's head, exploding in the sod several feet in front.

The mare reared, squealing in fright.

Alyse struggled to regain control of the horse.

Another red flame burst struck the grass.

The horse stumbled.

Alyse tumbled onto the grass, hit the ground hard, landing on her left shoulder. Pain streaked down her arm.

Livia cried out as she landed beside Alyse. Her staff flew from her hands. She scrambled onto her knees, grabbed Alyse's left wrist, and yanked. "Run!"

Alyse struggled onto her feet—just as a sword-wielding brigand stopped beside them. Shock of recognition made Alyse's body twitch. "Geoff!"

"Keep them there, Geoff!" a voice hollered from a distance.

Geoff turned and waved in recognition at the mage running toward them. Then he pivoted back to Alyse and Livia.

Ignoring her pain, Alyse stepped toward the mare that had calmed down after her scare and was munching on grass.

Geoff brought up his sword. "Stay away from the horse."

Tightness constricted Alyse's chest so hard it hurt. She had to win Geoff over before the mage arrived. If not, she and all her friends were as good as dead. "Listen, Geoff," Alyse said, clipping her words, "if you help us escape, I guarantee you refuge with my uncle in The Marches. Do you really want to waste your life here as a brigand? You deserve better than that."

Geoff glowered. "I was expelled unjustly."

"Yes, you were. Help us escape, and we'll help you start a new life as a legionary in my uncle's legions."

Geoff's brows narrowed, uncertainty clouding his eyes. "How can I trust your word?"

"Geoff, you know me." Her heart slammed madly against her ribs. "I've always treated you fairly. I even defended you when my great-grandmother expelled you."

Alyse flicked her gaze toward the mage who was just a staff length away. "I pledge my word."

Livia leaned toward Geoff, her body stiff with tension. "For the love of One Goddess. Help us!"

The mage stopped beside Geoff, puffing from running. "Good work. Palquo wants to give 'em special treatment."

A low growl rumbled in Geoff's throat. Turning, he thrust his sword into the mage's belly.

The man yelped, eyes round as saucers.

Geoff yanked the blade out, and the mage folded onto the grass, blood turning it from green to red.

"I'm with you," Geoff said. "I hate it here."

Cheering and laughter caused Alyse to look toward the brigands' camp. Kate, Jade, Yall, and Magnus were fighting ten or twelve outlaws while others brigands stood around, whooping and hooting and egging on their compatriots.

Anger swept through Alyse's chest. To them, the deadly, lopsided contest was entertainment. She switched her gaze to the woodpiles. The height of the cut firewood had been reduced to waist level because brigands pushed it into the passageway. Men and woman crowded around both sides and just outside the entrances, guffawing and prancing as they toyed with Rill, Troy, and Freya. Alyse's anger turned into a tidal current. The three of them were fighting for their lives while the outlaws acted like kids on a lark.

Geoff fetched Alyse's horse. "Lady Alyse, you did treat me fairly. All your life you did." He shot a worried glance at the fighting. "But I won't abandon Freya." He passed the reins to Alyse. "Leave now. Good luck."

Alyse rubbed her shoulder as the pain began fading. She had promised Geoff a new life, but he refused to abandon Freya. He was about to march willingly to his death because he preferred to fight and die beside his friend.

Adrenaline began flowing through Alyse's body, slowly at first, then surged, drowning her fear. She extended her hand to Geoff. "Give me your dagger."

Geoff's brows plunged into a puzzled frown. "Huh?"

"Your dagger."

Geoff slipped the blade out of its sheath and handed it to her. "What are you going to do?" But from the expression on his face, he'd already guessed.

Determined, Alyse met his stare. "I won't abandon my friends, either."

"My thinking exactly," Livia said, her blue eyes hard. "Uncle Deuth told me Illusion magic is worthless. Well, I'll show you it's not."

"How?" Alyse asked.

"By creating a distraction."

The three of them raced back toward the brigands' camp.

Escape

RILL STAGGERED AGAINST THE pile of unsplit logs as kindling tumbled into the passageway. One piece struck his knee. Sharp pain flashed through it like a bolt of lightning.

The brigands hooted, jeered, and catcalled.

Rill chanced a glance at Freya and Troy. Split wood littered the space where the two had been standing, but they appeared uninjured.

An outlaw leaned over the now low wall of wood and jabbed her sword at Troy.

Troy knocked it aside with his staff. Then, reversing the staff, smashed the orb against her head.

Yelping in pain, she staggered sideways and collapsed.

The bandits nearby pranced around her, sneering and snickering.

Freya dodged a spear thrust, yanked the spear from the man's grip, and tried to spit him with it.

He dodged.

But not fast enough because the blade sliced through his side.

The onlookers chortled.

Sudden movement from the corner of his eye snapped Rill's attention to the opening he was defending. A brigand was rushing through it, sword upraised for a strike. But he tripped on a piece of firewood. Before the man could regain his balance, Rill thrust his sword into him.

Then a woman stepped through the entryway.

Rill started toward her.

She quickly backed out.

Grim satisfaction settled in Rill's chest. The outlaws were learning that toying with them wasn't the fun and games they'd been expecting.

Troy paused to catch his breath while Rill parried the sword a man thrust at him from the other side of the cordwood pile. The attacker lurched back before Rill could thrust home.

"At least Livia and Alyse got away," Troy said.

"Yeah," Rill replied. "Now we gotta get away too."

"How do you expect to do that? We're surrounded."

"You're surrounded," a voice echoed in falsetto. "Surrounded. Surrounded. Surrounded."

The words were followed by mocking laughter from other bandits.

The urge to shove the split wood at the brigands flared in Rill's head.

Troy walked over to Rill, picking his way through the fallen wood. He spoke in a whisper. "We have to do something."

"I know," Rill said, his voice low and his focus fixed on the entryway at his end of the two piles. "Not unless we wanna die. And I sure don't. But if I hafta die, I refuse getting stuck in here like a pig in a pigpen. I wanna go out fighting." He paused. "And we *are* gonna die."

"I know," Troy said, resignation in his tone. "But at least we put up a good fight."

Rill's chest suddenly felt lighter as he accepted his fate. Then he stiffened as an idea crept into his mind. "It ain't over yet."

"What do you mean?"

"We'll create a distraction."

Troy frowned. "How?"

Rill pointed at the two cabins. "You'll set them on fire with Fireball spells."

"Their mages' charms might contain Water spells."

Rill gave a dismissive shrug. "Let's hope they don't."

Troy bobbed his head in acknowledgment. "Dying fighting in the open is better than dying cooped up in here."

Rill grinned, projecting a jauntiness he wished he felt. "We'll give 'em something to remember."

Swords clashed behind Troy. Freya stumbled backward and tripped over a piece of kindling. Her sword flew from her hand as she bumped against the stack of uncut logs.

Troy rushed back to defend the opening.

Booted feet treaded on wood behind Rill.

Rill spun around.

Two brigands had advanced a few feet through the opening. One of them motioned Rill forward with his fingers, a mocking grin on her face.

Suddenly terrified screams erupted from the outlaws surrounding the woodpiles. "Rattlesnakes! Rattlesnakes! Rattlesnakes!"

A multitude of rattling noises filled the air on all four sides.

"Watch out!" a panicky voice hollered. "It's gonna strike!"

"One Goddess preserve us!" someone yelled hysterically. "They're all over the place!"

Behind the two outlaws who were facing Rill, four rattlers—one of them at least three feet long—slithered through the gap. They stopped, as if assessing the situation, then coiled.

Suppressing his own stab of fear at seeing the snakes, Rill grinned at the brigands. "There's some rattlers behind you."

The beads on the snakes' tails vibrated.

An outlaw spun around. "Goddess in Elustra!" he shrieked. "There's four of 'em!"

Dropping their swords, both bandits scrambled over the cordwood pile to the opposite side.

A multitude of booted feet pounded on turf as the brigands fled, scattering in all directions.

Uncoiling, the snakes slithered over the cut timber toward Rill.

Rill's heart shot up his throat, and he slowly backed away, fearful each step might provoke a snake to strike. He started when he bumped into someone's back.

Troy's back.

Rill risked a glance over his shoulder. Troy and Freya stood side by side facing the other entrance, watching two rattlesnakes glide toward them over the pieces of cut wood.

"One Goddess Almighty," Troy said, eyeing them fearfully.

Rill's gaze snapped back to the snakes facing him. The three-foot one, which was in the lead, stopped on two slabs of wood and curled.

"I got four here," Rill said as he resheathed his sword and snatched up his bow. "And one's gonna strike."

The snake rattled the beads on its tail. Troy turned, muttering a curse.

Rill shot an arrow, which passed through the rattlesnake as if it didn't exist and lodged in the wood with a *thump*. "Holy Weavers!" Rill whispered.

"Incenbolt!" Troy's fire bolt streaked through the snake and set the wood beneath it on fire.

Unharmed, the snake continued its rattling, even while the fire began consuming the wood it was curled on.

The color drained from Troy's face. "The flames aren't affecting it!"

Unwinding, the rattler passed through the flames. The other three followed. The large snake stopped within striking distance of Rill, and curled. The others halted on either side and wound their coils. Then all four shook their rattles.

Rill sneaked a look at Freya.

Her body stiff as a pole, she was staring at the two rattlers that had entered from her end and were coiling in front of her.

Rill flicked his eyes back to the four snakes. Their rattling seemed to increase in volume. Rill's mouth had become so dry he couldn't swallow. And when he spoke, he couldn't control the panic in his voice. "How can we kill something that can't be killed?"

"Because they're illusions, you dummies," a familiar voice said.

Rill's gaze snapped frontward, just as someone appeared at the opening. Livia!

"I cast them," she said, pride in her voice. Then her tone changed to urgency. "Come on! We have to help the others." Without waiting for a response, she darted off.

"Let's go!" Rill said.

Troy and Freya charged out of the woodpiles and joined Rill. Then, stopping abruptly, Troy cast a Fireball spell on the stable. The huge ball of fire exploded through the double doors in a burst of orange-red flames, scattering pieces of burning wood in all directions. Immediately, the flames began to greedily devour the structure. Inside, horses snorted and squealed and pounded their hooves frantically against their wooden stalls. Their pitiful sounds tore through Rill's heart like a jagged arrowhead.

Rill seized Troy's arm and jerked him around. "What did ya set the stable on fire for?"

"You said we needed a distraction."

"I said the cabins, *not* the stable."

Troy yanked free, then cast Fireball on each cabin. The fireballs punched through the front walls and set the buildings on fire. Troy turned back to Rill. "*Now*, are you satisfied?"

Rill resisted the urge to punch him in the face. "No! The horses are gonna get burned alive. We gotta save 'em."

Troy blew out a dismissive breath. "Let the brigands do that. Saving our own lives is more important than saving horseflesh." He swept his arm across the landscape, taking in the burning cabins and stable. He grinned at Rill. "And it looks like none of their charms contain a Water spell."

"Come on," Rill said, the two words seething with disgust. "We hafta help the others."

Rill had hardly begun running when he spotted Livia. He skidded to a stop. She had just cast a Rattlesnakes spell on the outlaws who were fighting with Kate, Jade, and Yall. The crowd of bandits who had been watching and cheering their compatriots on just moments ago had dissolved, like snow melting under a hot sun, as they raced in a desperate attempt to save their cabins and rescue their horses. But Kate, Jade, Yall, and their outlaw opponents were so focused on slashing and parrying one another that they failed to notice the onlookers' flight or the huge number of rattlesnakes winding their way toward them through the green grass.

Rill cupped his hands around his mouth. "Rattlesnakes! Flee before they strike!"

Both sides paused.

The bandits spotted the snakes first, and fled.

Then Kate, Jade, and Yall noticed them. Horror spread across their faces. Blood-covered swords in hand, they backed away slowly, as if fearful that a quick movement might provoke an attack.

"They're illusions," Livia called out. "They can't hurt you."

Rill could see his companions' chests sink in as they sighed in relief. Then their shoulders wilted as they watched the snakes slide over their own boots and the boots, legs, and chests of dead and wounded bandits.

Livia ran up to the backwatchers. "Are you all right?"

"We are now," Kate said, drawing her booted foot away from a tardy snake that was about to glide over it.

Rill's gaze took in Kate's and the other backwatchers' slashed and bloody clothes. Despite their appearance, none of them seemed to have serious wounds.

Then another sight caught his attention. A half spear's throw beyond, oblivious to the chaos around them, Magnus and Palquo were fighting with dagger-tipped staffs. Livia cast Rattlesnakes on them, but neither mage appeared to notice the mass of angry rattlers wriggling around their feet. Rill peered more closely at Magnus. His movements were slower than usual, and the left side of his black tunic was soaked with blood. Rill nocked an arrow and shot at Palquo. He'd aimed at his chest, but Palquo moved suddenly, and the arrowhead pierced his arm.

Palquo staggered backward, caught his balance, and looked toward Rill. Then his eyes opened wide when he spotted the burning buildings and his band members hastily leading panicky horses from the barn and hurling buckets of well water in what they must have known was a fruitless attempt to save the cabins and stable.

Rill set another arrow on his bowstring and drew the bow back for a second shot at Palquo. A shield dome suddenly enveloped Palquo just as Rill released the arrow. The barbed head bounced off the shield, but the shock of the impact made Palquo drop his staff and lurch backward. The shield moved with him, but the staff remained on the grass.

Livia darted toward the staff. "You won't be needing this," she said to Palquo. Scooping it up, she returned to Rill's side.

Troy cast a Fireball spell on Palquo. The powerful burst of flame knocked Palquo over, but he slowly rose to his feet uninjured, with the shield intact and Troy's first arrow still embedded in his shoulder.

"He's harmless now without his staff," Troy muttered and turned away.

Leaning heavily on his staff, Magnus hobbled toward Rill and his companions, a hand pressed tightly against his side wound. Blood from another wound, which appeared less, stained the front of his tunic.

Rill flung an anxious look at the brigands, then at Magnus. "Can you move any faster?"

"Not much." Magnus winced from pain. "The bastard had a spring-blade staff. Whacked me first with the orb. Then, when I was off-balance, the blade popped out, and he stabbed me."

Rill and Magnus joined their companions, who were gathered around a brigand with sand-colored hair, who appeared to be in his late teens or early twenties. He had a nasty gash in his leg, just above the knee. Someone had torn a strip from the bottom part of his pants and wrapped it around the wound, but blood was slowly seeping through. Kate and Freya helped him to his feet and then draped one of his arms around each of their shoulders.

"Who's he?" Rill asked as he kept a wary eye on the brigands who were working desperately to extinguish the three fires.

"A friend," Kate replied tartly. "And he's coming with us."

Troy scanned the area. "Where's Alyse?"

"Gone to fetch the horses," Freya said.

Impatience tugged at Rill. "Come on! Let's get goin'."

Rill headed out but at a slow pace to accommodate the two injured men. Kate and Freya followed behind him with Geoff, and Magnus walked alongside them, his hand still pressed over his wound. Everyone else followed behind them, and kept glancing over their shoulders to keep a close watch on the outlaws, who were still preoccupied with extinguishing the fires.

"I sure hope all the horses got out safely," Kate said to no one in particular.

Rill shared her desire.

When they were partway across the meadow, Alyse appeared at the tree line on horseback, leading the rest of the mounts by their reins. She trotted down the gentle incline to them. "I thought you might need these," she said, holding out the horses' reins.

Alyse began to dismount so she could inspect Magnus's and Geoff's wounds and seal them with healing hands, but Rill told her they had no time for that. Alyse grudgingly remained in the saddle. Because they were shy three horses, Magnus rode with Alyse, and Geoff with Livia, while Kate doubled up with Freya. Rill took the lead, guiding them back up the hill and through the woods the way they had come. After a while, when they reached the beginning of meadowland, Alyse drew rein and told Rill they had to stop so she could treat Magnus's and Geoff's wounds.

"They've lost a lot of blood," Alyse said. "If I don't stop the flow of blood with healing hands, they'll both bleed to death."

Irritation and urgency vied to dominate Rill. "And if we do stop, the brigands could catch up with us. They're probably on our trail now. And they ain't none too happy about us burning down their cabins and stable."

Alyse stared straight at him, her determined green eyes meeting his blue ones. "I don't want Magnus or Geoff to die."

Rill returned the stare with equal determination. "And I wanna get us outta here alive."

Alyse kept looking at him while her lips curled. "Except for Magnus and Geoff, that is."

Rill silently cursed her obstinacy, but he was responsible for everyone's safety. "We ain't stoppin'."

Alyse sent Troy a questioning look, silently asking for his support. But he disappointed her. "Rill's right," he said. "We can't afford to—"

"No," Livia said. "It's Alyse who's right. We can't abandon—"

"We're wastin' time talking." In his mind, Rill pictured the brigands, madder than a nest of disturbed yellow jackets, chasing after them at a furious pace. They knew the lay of the land far better than he did. And the shortcuts.

He urged his mare to move faster, but Alyse's next words made him rein in abruptly.

"You go. But I'm staying."

Anger at her nerve for opposing him exploded inside Rill. He twisted around in his saddle to face her. She had already dismounted and was easing

Magnus off her horse. Rill maneuvered his mare to Alyse and leaned down to grab her arm, which she pulled out of reach. "Damn it, I said—"

Livia guided her mare up to Alyse's, dismounted, and helped Geoff get down from the saddle. "They both need to be treated," she said as she gently lowered Geoff onto the grass. "Now." Then she opened a saddlebag, pulled out a spare pair of woolen pants, and began ripping long strips of material from one of the legs.

Kate dismounted and walked up to Rill. She gazed at him, hazel eyes hard and a hand on the grip of her sword. "We're staying here."

Rill glowered at her, his stomach bubbling, like lava in a volcano ready to erupt, because he seemed to be losing control of the band.

"No one's stopping you from continuing," Livia told him. "We can take care of ourselves. Besides, Kate's with us."

"She's wounded."

"They're superficial," Kate said. "I can still fight."

Rill glowered at her, gritting his teeth.

Magnus grasped Alyse's stirrup to steady himself, keeping the other pressed tightly against his wounded side, while the wet splotch on the front of his tunic slowly expanded. "Rill, in the time you've spent arguing about not stopping, Alyse could have tended Geoff's and my wounds." He winced. "We all have to stay united. If we don't, the brigands will pick us off piecemeal."

Rill's eyes met Alyse's, and he read granite-hard determination in them. "All right," he said reluctantly. "But be quick about it."

While Yall, Jade, and Kate kept a sharp lookout for pursuit, Alyse placed her hands on Magnus's and Geoff's wounds and staunched the flow of blood. Then she bandaged the wounds using the wool strips Livia had torn from the pant leg. Finally, she examined the wounds with her inner eye. Rill watched her work and, despite his recent irritation, found himself admiring her efficiency. When Alyse finished, she stood up and faced everyone. Magnus's side wound was serious, she told them, but the chest wound not so much. And Geoff's was less severe too. Lobbing an accusatory glance at Rill, she added that they'd both lost a lot of blood, which would prolong the healing process.

By midmorning, Rill was relieved when they finally arrived at the Red Oak Inn without incident. After everyone dismounted and tied their horses' reins to the hitching rings, Rill and Troy helped Magnus and Geoff out of their saddles and eased them onto the ground. The stableboy came dashing toward everyone, but Rill waved him away. Turning to his companions, he suggested they rest their horses for a while and then start back to Caldon.

"The day's still young," he told them. "And we gotta put as much distance as we can between us and the brigands."

"No." Troy pressed his lips together, brows furrowed, as his gaze bored into Rill's with an I-dare-you-to-challenge-me look. "We're all hungry, dirty, and tired. We need to rest, and the horses do too. Besides, Alyse hasn't finished treating Magnus and Geoff."

"Or us," Yall said. "We have wounds too. Or have you forgotten just because we're not bleeding all over the place like sliced pigs?"

Before Rill could respond, Freya announced that she and Geoff intended to leave for The Marches as soon as Alyse tended Geoff's leg wound. She finished by saying they would ride the horse she had taken from the brigands' barn. She patted the mare's neck. "She's mine, actually."

"The horse belongs to us," Troy said. "Spoils of war."

"No, she's my horse," Freya retorted. "She was given to me when I joined the band."

Hands on hips, Troy leaned toward her. "Wrong. The horse is replacing the one the outlaws took from Lady Alyse. And they still owe the Dejunes one more horse to replace Kate's."

A storm of anger blew across Freya's face. "I didn't steal any Dejune horses. Besides, Geoff has a leg wound and can't walk very well."

"Then get him some crutches."

Freya's jaw tightened, and she started toward Troy. "Why, you—"

"Stop, both of you!" Alyse's lips compressed into a tight line. She untied Freya's mare from the hitching ring and stomped over to Freya. "If Troy wants the horse to belong to my family, fine. It's ours." She passed the reins to Freya. "Now it's yours."

"Hey!" Troy said, his voice raising several octaves. "That's not yours to give."

Alyse wheeled toward him. "You just said the horse belongs to my family. So I'm giving it to Freya as a reward for rescuing Kate and me." She paused and looked Troy in the eye. "Spoils of war."

Troy swatted her words away with a flick of his wrist. "No, that horse—"

"At ease, Little Brother," Livia said, adding an exasperated eye roll. "Alyse's horse is hers to give. End of story. And I'm buying a horse from the innkeeper for Geoff." She gave Troy a long stare, her features melting into disappointment. "Freya and Geoff helped save Alyse's and Kate's lives. Can't you be generous to them for that?"

Livia's words must have struck home because Troy's face turned red. He swallowed. "All right."

Livia sent him a tight smile. "Thanks."

Troy drew in a deep breath and held it, as if he were putting a damper on his anger, and then expelled it. "So it's settled. Geoff and Freya will leave for The Marches today. And the rest of us will spend the night here at the inn and head for home tomorrow."

"Wrong," Alyse said. "The *four* of us are leaving today for The Marches. Kate and I are going too."

Rill felt as if she had punched him in the belly, and it took a moment for him to catch his breath. Not bringing Alyse back could set Lord Deuth against him and jeopardize his plans to become a mage. He opened his mouth to object, but Troy beat him to it.

"You're *what*?" Troy said.

Alyse folded her arms across her chest, her posture radiating defiance. "Kate and I are leaving with Freya and Geoff. You don't think we came all this way—and endured being captured by the brigands—just to go back home, do you?"

Troy's gaze jumped all over the place—from Alyse to the horses, to the inn, to the stable—and finally back to Alyse. "The Marches? What . . . what in Goddess's name do you think we came all this way for?"

"To bring us home as prisoners."

"No!" Troy smacked the butt of his staff on the ground. "To bring you home as my betrothed."

Alyse threw her hands up in frustration, then leaned into him. "When will you get it through that thick skull of yours that I don't want to marry you?

I'm not even sure now if I want to have you as a friend." She paused to take a couple of deep breaths to get her emotions under control. "Marry Mora. She'll agree in a heartbeat."

"You know Great-Grandmother Ariella won't agree to that. Your grandmother won't, either." Troy lowered his voice and looked straight into Alyse's eyes. "And even if they would, I wouldn't."

"They don't have a choice." Alyse paused. "And neither do you."

Troy moved toward her. "Don't make me use force."

Kate quickly stepped between them. "I wouldn't advise that."

Freya strode up to Alyse's side and placed a hand on her sword's pommel. "Neither would I."

Troy's frown deepened.

Yall and Jade took up positions on either side of Troy, their hands on their swords' pommels too.

Rill stood apart from everyone, his horrified gaze hopping back and forth from one hostile group to the other while the tension between them mounted, like a longbow being drawn to the breaking point. Within moments, he knew, the longbow would snap and both groups would be fighting. Panic gushed through him. He'd come to rescue Alyse, not to get into a bloody fight with her and her friends.

"Can't we settle this peacefully?" he asked.

"That's up to Alyse," Troy replied, his eyes not leaving hers. "But I'll tell you this. I'd rather die here in an honest fight than shame my family, my ancestors, the future generations of Estatis, and myself by returning home without her." His gaze snapped to Rill, and his brows formed a frown. "Time to choose sides, Apprentice."

Rill hesitated, torn between loyalty to Alyse and loyalty to the Estatis. But he couldn't abandon his dream of becoming a mage. Drawing in a deep breath, he reluctantly positioned himself beside Troy. The disappointment that rippled across Alyse's face tore into him like a jagged-edged dagger.

Magnus's pain-filled voice spoke behind Rill. The mage had managed to pull himself onto his feet and was gripping the stirrup iron of Rill's horse. "Using force in this particular situation will only make things worse. Let's all of us be reasonable—"

"I'm through with being reasonable!" Troy said. "And I'm through with letting Alyse play me like a fool. By now, the whole of Caldon knows she ran away to avoid marrying me."

"That's quite an exaggeration."

Troy's anger-laden tone deepened with determination. "She's going back."

Dread infused Rill, making it hard for him to breathe. Troy was going to actually fight! His heart screamed against what was about to happen, but his mind ordered him to obey.

Then Livia stepped between the two groups and faced her brother. "Magnus is right, Troy. Force isn't the answer. Let Alyse go to Leoc. She'll come back eventually."

Troy's response shot out of his mouth like an explosion. "No!"

"Please!" Livia said.

She grabbed hold of her brother's arm, but he jerked it free with a force that made her stumble.

"Stop!" Alyse yelled.

Her fierce command made everyone freeze in place.

Nostrils flaring, she glowered at Troy. "I'll go back."

Grim faced, Troy gave a curt nod. "Good."

"But I won't marry you."

Troy's expression turned even grimmer. "We'll see about that."

Alyse blew out a snort of contempt. "You're too blind to see *anything*."

The apprehension that had been building up in Rill slowly drained. He was careful to avoid glancing at Alyse. She probably hated him by now. He wondered if Livia might, too, because she had sided with Alyse so strongly in the confrontation. For just a moment, he wished he'd never become involved in the rescue. But he quickly rejected the thought. If he hadn't, they probably wouldn't have discovered the brigands' hideout, and Alyse and Kate would probably have been killed.

The confrontation resolved, Troy told the stableboy to put their horses up for the night.

Before leaving the day before, Magnus had ordered Deek to keep their two bedrooms available for the next two days. Alyse treated Magnus's and Geoff's wounds in her room, which she now would share with Livia and Kate.

Magnus, Rill, and Troy would sleep in their old room. And Yall and Jade would spend the night in the stable. "To prevent our two little birds from flying away during the night," Troy said rudely, which earned him a dirty look from Livia.

Around midafternoon, Rill and Kate accompanied Alyse as she went to the hitching post with Freya and Geoff to see them off. Alyse made one final attempt to persuade them to postpone their departure until the next morning. "Spending the night here will give Geoff more strength," she told her two former backwatchers. "And Deek told me there's an empty room available if you want it. I'll pay for it." But, eager to be off, they declined.

While the stableboy was bringing Freya's and Geoff's horses to them, Alyse handed Freya a letter of introduction to her uncle, which urged him to take them on as legionaries. "And tell Uncle Leoc that I'm sorry I couldn't come with you."

Alyse's affection for her two friends increased Rill's admiration of her. But he figured he'd never again receive any from her because he had sided with Troy about bringing her back to Caldon. The realization saddened him.

That evening at supper, Alyse ate in stony silence, refusing to speak with anyone but Kate and Livia. She appeared to have little appetite, too, and mostly toyed with the chunks of meat in her bowl of pork stew. A few times Rill felt her frigid, green eyes on him, and each time a chill rippled down his spine. Once, he tried to thaw the icy wall she had erected between themselves by attempting to make conversation, but she patently ignored him. Her rejection left him with an empty feeling even though he'd been expecting it.

Early the next morning, the group headed west for Caldon, Magnus riding double with Yall. Troy made Alyse and Kate ride in the middle of the group as if he feared they would escape the first change that came their way. Rill rode in the rear, alongside Livia. Alyse sat stiffly erect in the saddle. Rill considered riding up alongside her and trying to break her silence again but feared another rejection.

Kate imitated Alyse's posture. Watching Kate's back, which she held rigid as a mage's staff, Rill wondered what kind of reception she would receive from the Dejunes when she arrived home. She'd probably be expelled, and she'd become a rohan. The prospect pricked Rill with sorrow. Then he wondered how Jedd would react. Jedd and Kate had become friends when they had fought together defending him—Rill—and Alyse during the attack on the One Goddess Temple. Would Jedd hold him responsible for Kate's expulsion? Rill hoped not, but feared he would. Rill expelled a frustrated sigh. He'd had no other choice than to support Troy, not if he wanted to remain Lord Deuth's apprentice.

The group rode at a leisurely pace, passing wooded hills, meandering rivers, and open fields, sprinkled with farms and studded with thick stands of woods. Alyse and Kate's riding skills impressed Rill because, used to a pampered life, few noblesse or backwatchers could ride well. That was evident from the poor way the others were posting, having trouble rising and falling in their saddles in time with their horses' gate. Rill also kept his eye on Magnus. The mage's side wound made it difficult for him to stay in the saddle. Yet Magnus soldiered on. Alyse must have noticed his suffering, too, because in the late morning she insisted they stop to rest at a three-way crossroads surrounded by a fringe of grass that bordered a huge expanse of woods.

Hot sunlight burned down on the dusty road, and birds fluttered from branch to branch in the trees, chirping merrily, and a brook babbled over rocks. While the others rested, Yall and Jade took the horses to the stream for water. Alyse and Kate sat on the other side of the intersection by themselves, their backs resting against a thick tree trunk, talking in voices that didn't carry across the road.

Rill sat down beside Livia, who seemed to be lost in thought. He looked across the dirt lane at Alyse. Guilt for his decision to side with Troy in yesterday's confrontation swirled around inside him, like dirty water that couldn't find a drain hole. He had to make her understand why he had done that. And the longer he watched her, the stronger the urge grew. Finally, his heart thumping like a frightened rabbit's, he crossed the road and asked the girls if he could join them. Kate hurled him a nasty glare, but Alyse hesitated, then nodded curtly. Propping his staff against the tree, Rill settled down in the grass beside Alyse. He chewed on his lip, working up the courage to speak.

"I . . . I hope you ain't angry with me . . . ya know . . . umm . . . for siding with Lord Troy yesterday," he said. "But I didn't have no choice." Alyse responded by folding her arms and looking past him, which increased his nervousness, making more words spill out of his mouth. "Really. And I didn't have no choice coming here with him. Lord Deuth ordered me to."

Unfolding her arms, Alyse twisted toward him, her lips pressed together into a tight, thin line. "You did have a choice."

"Honest, I didn't. If I refused, Lord Deuth wouldn't let me be his apprentice no more."

"Those were your choices. Refuse or obey. You chose obey."

Her harsh words unnerved Rill. "But you don't understand—"

"Oh, I understand full well. You want to become a mage at any cost. No matter who you injure. You beat up innocent merchants so they'd sign over the majority ownership of their businesses to the Estatis."

"'Cause they didn't pay back their loans."

Alyse spoke past him. "You battered that poor man, Dayson Florens."

"But he—"

Alyse scrambled to her feet and stood over him, hands on hips, outrage blazing in her eyes like two green fireballs. "You cracked his skull and broke his arm. He was my patient. I saw what you did, with my own eyes. Lucky for him the healer in his neighborhood One Goddess Temple sent him to me. Otherwise, he'd be dead."

The unjustness of her remark sparked Rill's anger. He jumped to his feet and met her eye to eye. "He owed a debt."

"The Estatis stole his business by giving him a loan they knew he couldn't repay. That's how they operate to become richer. That's how a lot of the noblesse operate. And, in case you didn't know, they also make loans to farmers and then take possession of their farms when they can't pay them back."

"I don't believe that."

"Then you'd better start believing because I saw it firsthand. They gave a poor farmer a loan. They knew she couldn't repay it because her children had been conscripted for the war. So the noblesse lender took over the farm and then kicked the family out—"

"'Cause they couldn't repay the loan, if what you say is true. And I ain't sayin' it is."

The vein in Alyse's neck pulsed. "It's because the farmers' kids can't work the farm because they're off fighting the Goddess-damned war against Gaetan."

Her accusations made Rill's chest tighten. He pinched his lips together. "Well! I see it ain't no good talkin' to you 'cause you can't see reason."

Alyse leaned toward him, arms stiff at her sides and hands clenched. "That's why you broke up with your family and your cousin, Jedd, isn't it? Because they couldn't 'see reason.' Or maybe because they'd told you you'd turned into a common thug."

A heavy feeling suddenly settled in Rill's stomach. "How do ya know about Jedd?"

"Everyone knows," Alyse said. "It's not just the talk of The Kings. It's the talk of The Citadel too. Jedd is Tor Euland's nephew after all. And many back-watchers still respect Tor."

Rill's throat tightened as if it were stuffed with wool, preventing him from speaking.

"Maybe I shouldn't have invited you to join us after all," Alyse told him. "We'll just argue. And you know what? Right now I don't feel like arguing."

Rill cleared his throat uncomfortably as guilt nipped at him. "Well," he said awkwardly, "I just wanted ya to understand why I sided with Lord Troy yesterday."

"I already understood the reason." Alyse looked scornfully at him. "Because you prostituted yourself to the Estatis in return for a charm and staff."

Blowing out a breath of bitterness, Rill glanced across the road at his lounging companions. Jade had rejoined them from the stream, the four mares watered and their reins tied to nearby tree branches. And Yall was returning with the remaining horses.

"I guess I ain't wanted here," Rill said.

"You guessed correctly," Alyse replied tartly.

Just then a sharp *crack* sounded in the woods somewhere behind Rill. A thin, orange-red bolt flashed past his head, crossed the road, missed Yall, and struck one of the horses in the flank.

Then chaos erupted.

CHAPTER 9

Attack at the Crossroads

THE HORSE REARED, EMITTINGa pain-filled squeal, and keeled over dead.

Surprise jolted Alyse to her feet as brigands charged out of the woods behind her, yelling and waving swords, battle-axes, and spears. Just as quickly, Kate was on her feet, sword out, and her body shielding Alyse.

Alyse's first instinct was to flee, find somewhere to hide.

A spear whizzed past her cheek, burying its head in a tree trunk with a solid *thwonk*.

The sound of iron against wood echoed in Alyse's head and set her blood boiling. First she'd been captured by the brigands. Then she'd been rescued. And now more brigands.

Battle frenzy seized Alyse. They wouldn't take her captive again. She'd had enough.

Alyse yanked out the spear. She might not be able to throw it, but she sure as Shelar could stick someone with it.

Nearby, on one side, Kate was crossing swords with an attacker. On the other side, just a spear length away, Rill had discarded his staff to engage a bandit in a sword fight. Across the road, Troy and the others were battling a large group of women and men who had attacked them from the woods on their side. She recognized some of the attackers.

Palquo's band.

Alyse whirled around at the crunch of boots running across dry leaves behind her.

An outlaw raced toward her, sword raised for the kill.

Alyse lunged at her with the spear.

The woman tried to avoid the thrust. But she was running too fast to maneuver to dodge the blade, and spitted herself on the spearhead.

The impact knocked Alyse over.

She scrambled back onto her feet. Nearby, a second attacker had joined the first one fighting Rill. Their backs to Alyse, step by step, they were forcing Rill backward toward the road. Alyse snatched the dagger from the sheath of the woman she'd killed and flung it at one of the men, just the way Kate had taught her. The knife tore into the man's back with a dull *thud*. He staggered and collapsed onto the leaves.

Alyse glanced toward Kate. Her cousin was defending herself against three attackers. Setting a booted foot on the chest of the woman she'd killed earlier, Alyse wrenched the spear from her chest and sprinted toward Kate. The brigands were so focused on Kate that they tuned out the sound of Alyse's running feet. Alyse shoved the spear into the side of the man wielding a battle-ax.

He stumbled, the movement whipping the spear shaft from Alyse's grip. Then he regained his footing and shot her a murderous look. "Bitch!"

Slowly, wincing from pain, he pulled out the spear, reversed the shaft, and moved toward Alyse on wobbly feet.

Alyse backed away while she cast a frenzied glance in search of a discarded weapon.

And backed into a tree trunk.

She looked at the man, her heart slamming against her rib cage, like an animal desperately seeking escape from a predator.

The man's lips curved into a cruel, vengeful smile as he made ready to thrust the blood-tipped spearhead into Alyse. "Die, bitch!"

Alyse started to move sideways to avoid the thrust.

Then Rill ran between them, ducked under the spear, and thrust his sword into the man's belly. As the outlaw started to fall, Rill yanked the spear from his grasp, pivoted, and flung it at one of Kate's opponents.

The spearhead buried itself in the man's back. He staggered against his fellow brigand, who lost his footing.

And Kate killed the brigand before he could recover.

Rill grabbed Alyse's arm. "Let's go!"

Alyse pulled away. "Not without Kate!"

"I'm here!" Kate said, suddenly beside her and breathing hard.

"Head for the horses!" Rill said.

All three sprinted across the lane.

From the corner of her eye, Alyse spotted Troy in a spell duel with unseen rohan mages. Troy kept casting offensive spells on them, but the mages kept foiling them with counter spells.

The horses whinnied in panic, spooked by the volleys of spells and counter spells. The ones Jade had hitched to tree branches were straining against their reins. Already one branch had broken, but a large knot near the tip of the broken end prevented the rein from sliding free. Yall, who hadn't had a chance to tie up the horses he had been leading, was digging his bootheels into the ground as he strained to keep hold of the reins.

Livia had helped Magnus to his feet and, with his arm around her shoulder, was supporting him as they half ran and half hobbled toward the horses. But the mage's shaky legs kept threatening to collapse beneath him.

Rill yanked the reins from Yall and managed to calm the horses. He yelled at Alyse. "Mount up!"

Defiance rose in her chest. How could she run off while her friends were still fighting? "Have Livia and Magnus double up and go first."

Rill opened his mouth to protest, but Alyse cut him short. "Do as I say!"

Thrusting the reins at Alyse, Rill helped Livia climb into the saddle and then boosted Magnus up behind her. Alyse watched, her heart beating in triple time. After what seemed like forever—while swords clashed and spells cracked all around them—Rill finally smacked the mare's rump, and the horse took off up the road heading west.

Rill grabbed another pair of reins from Yell, then nodded at Alyse. "Your turn."

Alyse stepped back from him. "The others go first."

Rill thrust the reins at her. "You're more valuable."

Alyse clenched her hands while hot anger gushed through her body. "I'm not someone's jewel that has to be protected. And I'm not leaving until everyone else is safely away."

Rill glared at her.

Alyse leaned toward him. "Just do it!"

One after another, Rill managed to get everyone onto the fidgety horses while Troy covered them by casting all sorts of offensive and defensive spells to counter the ones the brigand mages cast. The whole time, the hidden mages fought back, countering many of Troy's spells. But the defenders' continual moving about caused the spells that did get by Troy to miss their targets. Finally, only Alyse, Rill, and Troy were left with the last two horses. The mares fidgeted and pawed the ground, frightened and anxious to be off.

Troy cast several last spells, one right after the other in rapid succession. "Let's go!"

He scrambled into the saddle, then reached down and pulled Alyse up behind him. She wrapped her arms around his waist.

Rill waved him on. "Get goin'! I'll be right behind ya."

Troy kicked his heels into the horse's flanks, and the mare took off like an arrow shot from a bow.

Alyse glanced over her shoulder and gasped in horror.

His heels grinding into the dusty road, Rill was straining against his horse's reins, trying to control the panicky mare. Indistinct figures, many on horseback, flittered west among the trees and bushes, like apparitions, in an attempt to intercept their bolting quarry. But a trio was slipping on foot through the woods toward Rill.

Tension gushed out of Alyse's body when she saw Rill finally get the mare under control, spring into the saddle, and turn the horse's head west. But just as the mare was about to break into a gallop, a fire bolt flashed out of the woods and struck its shoulder.

The horse reared, squealing.

Rill toppled out of the saddle.

On Her Own

PANIC CLAWED AT ALYSE'S heart. "Rill's in trouble!" she screamed in Troy's ear. "We have to go back!"

"We can't!" Troy said.

"He'll be killed if we don't."

"And we'll be killed if we do." Troy paused, then heaved a half-hearted shrug. "He's on his own. It's every woman for herself."

Alyse's panic morphed into anger. Reaching past Troy, she grabbed the reins from his hands and jerked back hard. Startled, the horse reared, Alyse slipped out of the saddle and landed on the ground. She scrambled to her feet.

"Are you crazy?" Troy shouted as he struggled to control the mare. He grabbed for her arm. "Get back up here!"

Alyse scurried away. "I'm going to help Rill!"

"He's as good as dead!"

"Not if we help him!"

The rapid drumming of hooves on dirt penetrated Alyse's consciousness as Yall galloped back to them. Reining in his horse, he pointed frantically at the woods. Mounted brigands were turning from apparitions into solid beings. "Lord Troy, we have no time to lose. Let's go!"

Troy extended his hand to Alyse again. "Get up here!" he shouted, his tone frantic.

Alyse stepped farther away. "After we help Rill!"

Troy hesitated for a long, heart-thumping moment, fear and resolution fighting for dominion of his face. Then, turning his horse's head west, he dug his heels savagely into the animal's flanks and bolted away.

Yall raced to catch up.

Alyse ran toward Rill. He was on his feet now, sword in hand, facing three outlaws who were emerging from the trees. One carried a staff. But instead of closing in on him, they stopped and jeered. Alyse wondered what they were waiting for as her legs pumped beneath her like pistons. Then a figure materialized from the among the trees behind them. Alyse stopped short as fear's talons dug their pointed tips into her spine.

Palquo!

Palquo joined the other brigands, then pointed at Alyse and muttered something to them. Their spiteful laughter flew across the air to Alyse. Then Palquo aimed his staff at Rill.

"Palquo, no!" Alyse yelled, and broke into a burst of speed, running faster than she ever thought she could.

Rill dodged to one side just as a fire bolt shot out of the crystal orb in Palquo's staff. But he didn't move fast enough because a thin, orange-red flame burned into his side. Rill howled in pain and staggered backward. Palquo cast another fire bolt that seared Rill's thigh. The leg gave way beneath him and Rill collapsed.

The bandits chortled as they watched him writhe and moan.

Palquo pointed his staff at Rill again.

Alyse skidded to a stop on the dirt road beside Rill. Rage at the brigands and fear for Rill's life rushed through her like a gigantic tidal surge. Instinctively, she extended her arm, palm out, toward the outlaws while she pictured them flying backward. Her breath caught in her throat when a familiar sensation stirred in her solar plexus. In a fraction of a heartbeat, it gushed into her pelvis, down her arm, and exploded out of her palm. An invisible force struck all four bandits, hurling them backward through the air as if they were a child's dolls. Three, including Palquo, crashed against trees or were flung into bushes. The fourth, the other mage, struck his head against a tree trunk. Alyse heard the audible *smack* of bone against wood from where she stood. All four bodies remained still.

Alyse dropped to her knees beside Rill. Palquo's first fire bolt had left a deep, gaping wound in Rill's side that was gushing blood. His thigh had a horrible gash too. The stench of burned flesh made Alyse's stomach churn. *Focus! I have to act quickly to save him.*

Alyse had learned from the charm raid on her family's compound several months ago that the effect of a Fire Bolt spell on its victim depended on the caster's power. Fire bolts cast by less-powerful mages sometimes actually cauterized the wounds they made, which staunched the bleeding and increased the chances of recovery. But wounds caused by fire bolts cast by powerful mages remained open and bled until the injuries were sealed. Most healers couldn't work quickly enough to stop the blood flow before the victim bled to death. Alyse muttered an urgent plea to the One Goddess that she wouldn't be one of those.

Fortunately, the fire bolts had missed Rill's arteries, but dark-red blood was spilling steadily from the veins in both wounds. Placing her hands over the ugly, gaping side wound, Alyse summoned healing magic and focused on sealing off the veins while Rill's blood bled between her fingers and leaked out from under her palms. Time seemed to drag by without the stream slowing, and she feared her magic might not be strong enough to perform the task. Then, to her relief, the blood flow began to slacken, slowed to a trickle, and finally stopped.

Alyse yearned to collapse in exhaustion. Instead, she placed her bloody hands on Rill's leg wound and summoned healing magic again.

By the time Alyse had finished, she felt drained in a way she had never experienced before. She longed to lay down beside Rill, curl up into a ball, and let her consciousness fade into sleep. But she resisted the urge because she still had work to do. Setting her face resolutely, she carefully examined Rill's body with her inner eye. Fortunately, none of his vital organs were damaged, but a low-level malevolent energy emanated from both injuries. She wished she'd paid attention to how healers had treated her family's retainers who had been wounded by Fire magic during the attack on her compound. Then she kicked the thought aside. It was useless to berate herself for not doing it.

Rill's mare stood nearby and was squealing painfully. Alyse went to the horse and, after wiping her bloody hands on her pants, put a hand on the horse's cheek. "Poor girl. They hurt you too. Let me have a look."

When Alyse went to touch the mare's shoulder, the horse shied away. Eventually, though, Alyse's soothing tone and gentle manner calmed the mare so Alyse could inspect the injury. Alyse frowned. The wound was mostly cauterized. Her focus moved to the mage with the smashed skull. He must have cast the fire bolt on the mare and, obviously, was less powerful than Palquo. Alyse's heart skipped a beat as the thought slithered into her mind like a deadly serpent—perhaps a mage was still lurking in the woods, watching. Alyse cast an anxious glance at her surroundings but detected nothing amiss, except for the four bodies sprawled in the woods across the road.

Her nerves tightened, but she forced them to relax. She couldn't let fear immobilize herself.

Alyse eyed Palquo and the three other brigands, and then swept her gaze across the bodies of the brigands lying in the woods where she, Rill, and Kate had fought. One of the bodies moved, emitting a low moan. *I did that!* A ripple of horror passed through her, from head to toe. Then her throat clogged and her stomach cramped. Plopping onto her knees, she threw up, spilling the messy contents of her stomach onto the dirt road. Afterward, she wiped her mouth on her sleeve and drew in several long, ragged breaths.

The mare squealed.

"Sorry, girl," Alyse said as she shakily climbed to her feet. "I had to get my nerves under control."

While she spoke soothingly to the horse, Alyse sealed the veins that were bleeding. Then she examined the mare's injuries with her inner eye. Her brows crinkled into a puzzled frown when she didn't detect any lingering malevolence such as she'd seen in Rill. But there was no time to ponder that now. She had other worries.

Alyse bit her lower lip as her eyes jumped from Rill to the horse and back to Rill, and finally up the now deserted road leading westward.

What to do next?

She stared at Rill's body laying on the dirt road, betrayal stabbing her like a poisoned dagger. He had been her friend but had severed their budding friendship by coming with Troy to take her back as a prisoner to face an unhappy future. One part of her mind urged her to leave him where he lay. But the other part . . .

Heaving a sigh, she shook her head, bemused by her refusal to do the obvious. *The Five Sisters have woven strands of our tapestries together, Rill Larkin, whether we like it or not.*

Alyse chewed her lip as she sorted out her options. They were depressingly few. Go west to Caldon. But the brigands had pursued Troy and the others in that direction and would return that way. Besides, that road would take her back to the Estatis and an unwanted marriage to Troy. Go east and seek refuge at the Red Oak Inn. But she couldn't imagine Deek protecting her. Or go to her uncle's legionary camp in The Marches. But the distance was too far to travel with Rill, who was seriously wounded, and the horse, which had also been wounded. So that left her with one other alternative: going south. Alyse rubbed the back of her neck while she gazed up the road, which became narrower and narrower until it disappeared among the distant trees. She had no idea where it led, but what other option did she have?

Alyse went to the mare, which was waiting patiently nearby, and stroked its forehead. "I'm sorry, girl, but you can't take a rest just yet."

Alyse led the limping horse to Rill and tied the reins to a branch. She rummaged through the saddlebags and found a change of pants, cut the legs using Rill's dagger, and wrapped the cotton strips around his wounds and the mare's. Then she gazed at the crossroads while her mind flipped through alternatives, like a card player shuffling a deck of cards. The brigands could reappear at any moment, and she had to be gone when they did. But how to bring Rill with her? If she draped him over the saddle, the strain of movement might open his wounds and the jouncing of the horse limping might too. Besides, she doubted that she had the strength to lift his lifeless body high enough to even reach the saddle. Then her eyes latched on to a sapling near where the mare was munching a patch of grass by the edge of the road, and an idea burst into her mind like an explosion.

A drag sled.

Eagerly, she retrieved Rill's sword and hacked down and trimmed a pair of long saplings for the poles and shorter ones for cross supports. Then she scurried across the road to where the brigands lay. Besides the one with a broken skull, a second lay dead with a broken neck. Palquo and the fourth outlaw were still alive but unconscious. Palquo wore a shirt and vest, while the others wore tunics. Alyse hesitated for a moment. Then, drawing a determined breath and gritting her teeth, she stripped the tunics, vests, shirts, and pants off three of the bandits. But she took only the pants from the man with the smashed skull because she didn't relish the prospect of having his brain smeared on his tunic when she tugged it over his head.

Alyse started to leave but paused to look back at Palquo and the other mage. Sunlight bounced off the charms on their naked chests like a pair of deadly fishing lures. She went back to them, removed the charms from their necks, and cast them deep into the woods. She threw their staffs after the charms, but in a different direction. Then she took one of the outlaw's sheathed daggers from his belt and attached it to hers, and flung the remaining weapons into the woods.

Alyse returned to Rill and constructed a drag sled from the trimmed saplings and the bandits' clothes by sliding the poles through the tunics and buttoned-up vests to create a bed of sorts, making sure she put extra padding near where Rill's head would rest. Then she cut strips of material from the pants and used them to lash the cross pieces together. After unbuckling Rill's sword belt, she dragged him onto the sled and tied the opposite ends of the poles to the horse's saddle, using more strips cut from the brigands' pants. Finally, she tied Rill's sheathed sword to the bedroll behind the saddle and stuffed his belt and sheathed dagger into a saddlebag.

Alyse took one last look around and noticed Rill's staff still propped up against the tree, where they had been talking before the attack. She strode up to the tree, seized the staff, and hurled it deeper into the woods. Then she returned to the mare and rubbed its muzzle affectionately. "Please do this one last thing for me, and then you can rest."

The horse whinnied as if saying she would.

Alyse inhaled a huge lungful of air while her heart thumped against her ribs so hard she could hear the beating in her ears. "Here we go," she said.

Taking hold of the reins, Alyse began walking resolutely up the road, heading south.

CHAPTER 11

A Light in the Window

ALYSE WALKED ALONG THE dusty road through the woods. Her heart ached for the poor horse, which hobbled along beside her pulling Rill in the drag sled. She stopped frequently to rest the mare. Each time, her nerves twisted to the snapping point because she feared the brigands might burst into sight at any moment on the road behind her. But she feared losing the use of the horse more than confronting the outlaws. Without the mare, she would have to haul the drag sled herself, and she knew she couldn't lug it too far.

Every so often, travelers passed her, but none of them stopped to offer assistance. They merely glanced curiously at her as they rode or walked by. Apparently, people in these parts minded their own business.

Alyse stopped for a longer break in the early afternoon. She fed the mare from a half-empty feed bag tied to the saddle. "You're a good girl," she said, stroking the horse. "And when we finish this horrid adventure, I'll fill your belly with nice, juicy apples."

The mare must have understood because she nickered in reply.

Alyse ate some journey cakes she discovered in the saddlebags and washed them down with water from Rill's waterskin. Afterward, she explored Rill with her inner eye. She frowned to herself when she detected a slight increase in the malevolent energy.

After a while, Alyse emerged from the woods into open country. This area looked poorer than the others she'd passed through before being captured. Here the land was rocky, hilly, and barren, with occasional woods and streams, and dotted with ramshackle farms made from weathered wood and surrounded by low walls built from stones the farmers had cleared from their fields. Each farm had a few thin pigs rooting in an enclosure, one or two skinny cows, and some chickens pecking in the barnyard. Several also had a handful of scraggly sheep or goats, and a few had a pair of oxen whose ribs were outlined beneath their hides. In the fields, gaunt women and men and scrawny children dressed in threadbare clothes bent over vegetable gardens working and harvesting the paltry yields of First Fruits season. From time to time, a few glanced up with hard faces to watch Alyse plod by, leading a horse that was pulling a drag sled with an injured boy on it. But no one was curious enough to approach her.

Alyse stopped in surprise when she spotted her first villa farm. The place was huge—large enough to hold twelve or thirteen of the small, poor farms. She paused to squint at it, wondering what it was doing there, before continuing. As she trudged along, she passed more villa farms. Like the first, all the farmhouses, barns, and outbuildings were expertly constructed from solid timbers, and painted. Fat pigs rooted in fenced-off pastures and woods. Herds of plump cows munched on green grass. And well-fed sheep and goats grazed in fields of their own. Brooks babbled through the land, providing sustenance to crops and livestock. A few farmworkers, who were well clothed and appeared well fed, appeared to be overseers. But the women, men, and children who actually did the work were as scrawny and poorly dressed as the ones Alyse had seen toiling on the impoverished farms. She knew right away who owned these farms.

The noblesse.

Like the poor farmers, neither overseer nor worker was interested enough to walk to the road and ask her why she, a lone teenage girl, was leading a crippled horse that was pulling a wounded teenage boy on a drag sled. Perhaps the farmers were too downtrodden to wonder, and the overseers didn't care.

Toward midafternoon, Rill regained consciousness. Alyse stopped the mare, knelt beside him, and took one of his hands in both of hers.

Rill peered groggily at her. "W-where am I?"

Alyse smiled at him, her deep-green eyes tearing. "You're safe. That's what's important." She mentally berated herself for lying, but telling the truth—that evil magic lingered inside him—would be worse.

Rill struggled to sit up, and yelped in pain.

Gently, Alyse eased him back down onto the sled. "Go back to sleep, Rill. Everything will be fine."

Rill uttered a laugh that morphed into a moan. "That . . . that's supposed to be my line." He paused, then said, "Water. I'm thirsty."

Alyse gave him a few sips from the waterskin. "You need to rest now," she said as she pushed the stopper back into the spout.

Rill closed his eyes and fell back to sleep.

Alyse slogged on into the early evening. She passed several crossroads along the way, but the names on the signs pointed in directions that were unfamiliar. Where the road she was on led was just as mysterious, but at least it pointed in a straight direction, so she wouldn't get any more lost than she already was. Now, though, as the descending sun lit up the sky in multiple hues of yellows, oranges, and reds, anxiety wound its coils inside Alyse's belly. She had to find a place to spend the night, preferably under someone's roof. She needed to follow up on treating Rill and the mare. And she had to obtain more food because the journey cakes were almost gone. And even if they weren't, Rill required more wholesome nourishment than those flat slabs of bread to recover his strength and fight the malevolent energy that had attached itself to him like a tick.

"Lady," she prayed silently to the One Goddess, "please guide us to the right family."

By the time twilight had faded to dusk, and the sun had slid below the horizon, Alyse's stomach had twisted into a tight, painful knot of desperation. She refused to approach the villas because their owners might know her family, either as an ally or an enemy. Yet she feared throwing herself blindly on just any poor farm family for help. Instead, she trusted the One Goddess to send her a sign. But so far, all She had sent her was a bad feeling for every poor farm she'd passed.

Alyse choked back a sob. *Lady, why can't you help me?*

As dusk was folding into the nighttime sky, and desperation was chewing on Alyse's belly, like a cougar gnawing on a carcass, she happened upon another poor farm. The pale light of the half-moon showed vague silhouettes of a farmhouse, barn, and outbuildings that were smaller than many she had passed. Yet the warm, yellow glow from oil lamps in the unshuttered windows on either side of the farmhouse door sent her a peaceful feeling. She stopped and stood still, hesitant to walk down the narrow, dirt path to the farmhouse door.

Finally, she took a deep breath and gathered up her determination. "I hope you guided me here, Lady," she prayed, "because we're going in."

Her heart vibrating like a tuning fork, Alyse led the mare onto the dirt pathway.

Alyse had almost reached the farmhouse door when a menacing growl came from the shadows near the house. The horse shied, but Alyse gripped the reins tighter.

The growl turned into multiple barks.

The mare spooked even more.

Alyse pulled on the reins to prevent the horse from bolting, once or twice almost losing her footing.

Suddenly a huge, dark shape leaped out of the shadows and blocked her path. A menacing growl rumbled deep in its throat.

The horse snorted and trembled.

Fear churned in Alyse's stomach. She inhaled a few deep breaths in an attempt to calm herself down. Then, avoiding eye contact and keeping hold of the reins, Alyse slowly went down on her knees and spoke in a gentle voice. "Why, hello there, fella. What's your name? Barkie. That's what I'll call you. Because you sure do bark a lot."

The dog lunged toward her, barked, then scurried back. It kept repeating the action until it finally sat down in front of her. The dog barked a few more times, then fell silent.

Tentatively, Alyse stroked its head. "That's a good fella."

The dog rubbed against her.

Alyse scratched under its chin—

The farmhouse door banged open.

Light flared in the doorway.

Alyse blinked at the sudden explosion of brightness—and saw a tall, lanky man standing on the threshold. He held an oil lantern in one hand and a mean-looking sword in the other.

"Who's out there," he said, a challenge in his tone. "An' what did ya do to my dog?"

Alyse rose, one hand on the dog's neck and the other holding the mare's reins. "My name is Alyse. And, as you can see, I didn't do anything to your dog."

"Ya ain't done nothin'?" The man harrumphed. "Ya tamed the critter. That's whatchya done. And a tamed dog ain't no good against trespassers, brigands, and damned noblesse."

Alyse gulped down a huge lump of despair. He hated noblesse. The Lady had abandoned her. She pulled herself up straighter while her heart beat harder and faster. Convincing this man to give them shelter might make the difference between life or death for Rill. "I have an injured friend who requires attention. And we need a place to spend the night."

The man stomped toward her. A scrawny boy in his early teens trailed behind him, clutching a heavy war spear twice as tall as himself. The lantern light revealed the man's lanky frame. Alyse judged he was in his early fifties. The dog padded over to the farmer, who tapped its side with the flat of his sword.

"Mastav, ya let me down. Some guard dog you are! I should cut you up to make bear bait."

Mastav licked the man's hand.

"Well," the man said irritably, "let's see whatchya got here." He called over his shoulder. "Jenna, come on out! She says she's got an injured friend."

A woman emerged from the farmhouse carrying a second lamp. Black hair streaked with gray framed a lined, care-worn face. A girl, who appeared to be a few years younger than the boy, followed her. When the woman stopped beside the man, the girl peeked shyly at Alyse from behind the woman's skirt.

The farmer studied Alyse through hostile eyes. "Ya dress like a commoner. But ya sure don't talk like one." He moved the lantern closer to her. His eyebrows narrowed, making his forehead crinkle. "And ya got blood on them there clothes of yours."

Alyse's eyes watered, and her body trembled in the lamplight. She had to make the man help her. "I was captured by brigands." She nodded at Rill. "And my friend was wounded helping me escape."

The woman made no response but the man did.

"So you're gonna bring the damned brigands down on us now, are ya? As if we ain't got enough troubles already."

Alyse's heart plunged down to her feet, squashing all hope of assistance from these people.

"And you're noblesse to boot!" The farmer hawked and spat. "That means we got even more troubles." Grumbling, he went to the sled, held the lantern over Rill, and bent toward him. "What happened to him?"

"I told you. He was wounded helping me escape."

The farmer tapped Rill's bloody tunic with his sword. "Who's livery is that?"

Alyse's throat went suddenly dry. She paused for several heartbeats, dreading the man's reaction. Then she drew a deep breath, let it out, and said, "Estati."

The farmer's back arched up straight. "Estati!" He turned toward Alyse. "Damn the Estati! An' a plague on all them Goddess-damned noblesse." He cocked an eye at Alyse. "I'll wager that ain't no ordinary wound he's got, neither."

Despair swirled around inside Alyse. The encounter was turning out to be worse than she had ever imagined. But she would see this through. If she failed, it wouldn't be because she had been faint hearted. She straightened her shoulders and look the man in the eye. "That's right."

"Magic?" he asked.

"Yes."

"What kind?"

"Fire Bolt spell."

The lamplight glinted off the chain around Rill's neck. The farmer squinted suspiciously at it. Handing the sword to the boy, he gingerly lifted the chain out from beneath Rill's tunic, exposing the charm. "A mage, by Goddess! A damned mage."

The man's hate-filled rant finally broke Alyse's composure. "I've sealed off his veins. But he's still in danger of dying. For huwomanity's sake, I beg you to let us stay the night so I can tend to him properly. It could make the difference between life or death. And the horse needs healing too."

"For huwomanity's sake," the man said, mimicking Alyse's voice. "What does your kind know about huwomanity? We'd be better off if all you Goddess-damned noblesse and mages was dead." He pointed up the path to the road. "Take your friend and your horse and get outta here."

Alyse choked in despair."

For the first time, Jenna spoke. "Let me take a look at the boy."

"Ain't no need for that," the man said. "They're about to leave."

Jenna walked up to the farmer. "Oh, hush up, Dorn, and move outta my way."

Grumbling, Dorn stepped aside. Jenna knelt beside the stretcher and examined Rill by the flickering yellow light of her lantern. When she stood up again, she studied Alyse with stony eyes. "What's ya name?"

"Alyse."

"You ain't got no family name?"

Alyse swallowed. Her throat clenched so tightly at her fear of Jenna's response when she said "Dejune" that her saliva had a tough time going down. Then she chided herself. For better or worse, she *was* a Dejune. Throwing her shoulders back, she met Jenna's gaze full on. "My name is Alyse Dejune. Granddaughter of Jukka Bern, chief mage of Caldon. Niece of Leoc Dejune, Commander of the Eastern Army. I'm betrothed to Troy Estati, nephew of Deuth Estati—"

Dorn hawked and spat. "That's what I think of you Dejunes. An' all the other Goddess-damned noblesse too."

Alyse's heart quaked.

"Oh, hush up, Dorn," Jenna said, her eyes sticking to Alyse like a pair of flies on flypaper.

Dorn sputtered into silence.

Jenna raised her lantern to illuminate Alyse's face. "I asked for your family name, not your pedigree. An' if you're foolish enough to go around these parts sayin' all that, you'll make yourself a lot of enemies."

"Or end up dead," Dorn said.

Alyse's cheeks burned from the put-down.

Jenna nodded curtly at Rill. "You said you healed his wounds."

"No," Alyse responded, shaking her head. "I said I sealed off his veins so he wouldn't bleed to death. But I have a lot more work to do to save his life if"—she choked on the words—"if it's not already too late."

"You're a healer?"

"Yes."

"You're pretty young to be callin' yourself a healer."

Alyse grimaced. "And too inexperienced as well. I'm an apprentice healer at the One Goddess Temple in Caldon."

Jenna shot her an odd look. "In what neighborhood?"

"The Kings."

"You got a mentor?"

"Chief Priestess Sybil Raine."

Jenna's body stiffened, her eyes flying wide open, and Dorn uttered a surprised gasp. Alyse bit the corner of her lip, uncertain how to interpret their reactions.

"Does the name Hilbrand Wistlow mean anything to you?" Jenna asked.

Astonishment made Alyse gasp involuntarily. "I've never heard the name before."

Dorn snorted. "Can't even lie good neither, can ya. Some noblesse *you* are."

"Oh, hush up, Dorn." Jenna gazed at Alyse, her harsh expression softening. "I know you're sworn to secrecy. But Hilbrand's the son of a friend of ours."

Stunned, Alyse's mouth dropped open.

"An' we know about Ord and Ebar," Dorn added.

Confusion swirled in Alyse's mind with whirlwind force while Jenna waited patiently for a response. "I . . . I was never told Hilbrand's last name. But he had a gangrene leg. And I healed it . . . with the help of a much more powerful healer."

"Which his family is extremely grateful for," Jenna said.

Alyse touched Jenna's arm. "That knowledge is dangerous. If the trackers—"

"There ain't no trail that'll lead 'em here," Jenna said. "And if they do come and ask, we'll tell the truth. They were never here, and we don't know where they are."

Dorn cackled. "We got ways to deal with mind benders—"

"Dorn Grimie, hush up!" Jenna's stern face melted into a smile. "I'm Jenna Desfar. You're welcome here, Lady Alyse. Our home is your home for as long as you need."

Dorn bobbed his head. "That's right. No Grimie or Desfar ain't never turned away a friend in need."

He handed his lantern to Alyse and untied the strips of cloth that held the sled's poles to the mare's saddle.

Jenna turned to the boy. "Tolle, put down the spear and the sword and help your grandpa bring Lady Alyse's friend inside. Put him in your parents' bed." She laid a hand on the girl's shoulder. "Serin, honey, take Lady Alyse's horse to the barn and make her comfortable. Give her some hay and brush her down. But be careful around that nasty wound she has on her shoulder."

Jenna watched Serin lead the mare away, a look of absolute love on her face. The unfiltered emotion filled Alyse with wonder. No one in her family had ever looked at her that way. Not her parents, grandparents, great-grandparents, or sister. Not even Uncle Leoc. She envied Serin.

Jenna interrupted Alyse's thoughts. "Please come inside, Lady Alyse."

Alyse and Jenna followed Dorn and Tolle, who carried Rill into the kitchen and through a door on one side of the hearth into a small bedroom. The glow from Jenna's lantern revealed a nightstand beside a double rope bed with a straw mattress. Dorn and Tolle laid the sled on the wood-plank floor and carefully lifted Rill onto the mattress.

Dorn slipped Rill's charm off his neck. "He don't need this no more."

Alyse parted her lips to protest, then squeezed them shut. Dorn was right. The less magic, the better.

Dorn and Tolle left with the drag sled.

Jenna placed the lamp on the night table, then touched Alyse's shoulder. "Lady Alyse, there'll be food for you on the kitchen table after ya tend to your friend."

Alyse smiled her thanks. "Please call me Alyse. And I'll eat after I've also seen to my horse."

Alyse knelt beside the bed, conscious that Jenna had stayed to watch. Gently, she unwound the rough bandages from Rill's side and thigh. The veins were still sealed, but the raw, seared flesh had a sickly pallor and a faint odor that made her stomach lurch. She looked up at Jenna. "Can you bring me some water and soap? And do you have any clean cloths I can use for bandages?"

Jenna left to carry out her request.

Alyse explored Rill with her inner eye and bit her lip at what she sensed. The pallor and smell were caused by the lingering malevolence. Hopelessness squeezed Alyse's heart. How could she combat the unhealthy magic? She'd never heard of such a thing before. Did the spell reflect the spiritual embodiment of the caster? Had Palquo become evil? From the way he'd acted, he probably had. A sense of helplessness gripped Alyse as she applied healing hands to Rill's wounds again, knowing the treatment wouldn't help but hoping it would.

When Jenna returned, Alyse cleaned and rebandaged Rill's wounds. Afterward, she went into the barn to examine the mare. Serin had just finished rubbing her down and feeding her. Alyse asked Serin to take Rill's sword, bow, and quiver into the house, which she did after flashing Alyse a shy, tentative smile. Heaving a tired sigh, Alyse examined the horse with her inner eye. To her relief, the mare was recovering, with no sign of the malevolent energy. She was thankful for that.

Alyse returned to the farmhouse and slumped onto the bench at the trestle table near the hearth. The only light came from the fireplace, the lanterns in the two windows, and several candles scattered throughout the room. The rest of the room was obscured by shadows. Jenna, her back to Alyse, was returning a crock to one of the shelves that lined the side wall. The other shelves held wooden trenchers, earthenware mugs, dishes, and an assortment of clay storage crocks and jugs. Alyse glanced around at the rest of the room and its plain, simple furnishings. A spinning wheel stood near one of the front windows and a loom holding a partially completed blanket by the other.

Jenna went to the hearth and filled a trencher from a kettle hanging on a crane over the fire. She placed the food in front of Alyse, whose stomach growled when she inhaled the delicious aroma of chicken stew.

A few loaves of freshly baked bread were on the table, interspersed among several wide-mouthed wooden mixing bowls. Jenna cut a thick slab of the crusty bread and placed it beside the stew bowl. "Lucky for you, La . . . Alyse, that today was baking day."

Alyse smiled tiredly at her as she picked up the spoon. "Thank you."

Dorn watched her from the corner where he sat mending a harness. Tolle sat on the floor playing some kind of game while Serin gave instructions to a doll made of straw. Mastav lay curled up near the fire, snoring.

Serenity settled over Alyse like a warm, comfortable blanket. She wondered if Elustra, the Afterworld, was like this.

CHAPTER 12

The Strenga

AS RILL'S CONDITION GOT got worse and worse each day, a dark cloud of depression hovered over Alyse. Even though she knew applying healing hands wasn't working, she used that magic on Rill anyway, each time praying to the One Goddess and begging that She intervene. But if the One Goddess had heard, She was refusing Alyse's fervent requests. Jenna and Dorn expressed their concern every time Alyse came out of his bedroom. Sometimes after she answered, Alyse caught them exchanging that same silent message.

This morning, despair settled heavily in her chest as she left Rill's bedroom. After closing the door, she leaned against it, buried her face in her hands, and sobbed. Dorn had just come in from the field to fetch something, Jenna was spinning wool, and Serin was carding wool to separate the fibers so Jenna could spin them. Jenna motioned for Serin to leave, then crossed the rough-hewn floorboards with Dorn to where Alyse was weeping.

Jenna put an arm around Alyse's shoulder. "He's gettin' worse?"

Alyse looked at their blurry faces, and her throat thickened. "He's *dying*, and there's nothing I can do except watch him die." She drew in a huge, ragged lungful of air. "It's only a matter of days before . . ." She slumped against Jenna. "If only Priestess Sybil were here. Or Kendra. They'd know what to do. But me . . . I don't. All I can do is watch him die."

Sobs racked her body.

Gently, Jenna wiped tears from Alyse's cheek. "He means a great deal to you, don't he?"

"We've been through a lot together."

"Do ya love him?"

Alyse pulled back, and her tear-drenched eyes popped open in surprise. "Love him? No. But there's a . . . a connection between us. Between me, him, and his family. I think maybe the Five Sisters wove all of our tapestries together for some reason. But whatever that reason is, the Sisters don't care about it anymore."

Dorn frowned at his wife. "I think it's time."

Jenna nodded.

Alyse sniffed and wiped snot from her nose. "Time for what?"

Dorn motioned to Jenna. "You tell her."

Maybe it's time we visited Twalla," Jenna said.

"Who's that?" Alyse asked.

Jenna hesitated, then glanced at Dorn who motioned for her to continue. "A strenga."

Alyse's stomach lurched violently in horror as she stepped back and bumped against the latch on the bedroom door but was oblivious to the metal digging into her spine. "A strenga!"

Jenna started to put a hand on her shoulder, but Alyse moved sideways. Jenna sighed, firing a frustrated look at Dorn who arched his brows as if to say, "What did I tell ya?" She motioned for Alyse to sit down at the trestle table. Reluctantly, Alyse obeyed. Jenna and Dorn seated themselves across from her. Then, forearms on the table, Jenna leaned toward Alyse and asked, "What do ya know about the strengi?"

"They're evil and practice dark magic."

Dorn responded with a *humph*, which earned him a glare from Jenna.

"What else?" Jenna asked.

Goose bumps rose across Alyse's shoulders, like mushrooms popping out of the ground, as the horrid stories she'd been told as a child chased one another through her mind. "They practice their magic at night. They call on the dark powers of Shama, the Goddess of the Underworld, to work their spells."

Dorn did an eye roll.

"They sacrifice babies—"

Jenna held up a hand. "That's enough of those bogeywoman tales. Have ya ever met a strenga?"

"Of course not! But I've been told—"

"Lies."

Alyse felt as if Jenna had just punched her in the stomach. It took a moment for her to catch her breath. "What?"

"Lies told by the noblesse and the mages to stomp out their competition."

Alyse's brows plunged into a puzzled frown. "What competition?"

"Between healers."

Alyse's frown deepened. "What do you mean?"

"Strengi are healers."

Alyse drew in a quick breath while the base of her neck suddenly tingled with discomfort. She shook her head. "No! That's impossible."

An amused smile formed on Jenna's lips. "Then what are they?"

Alyse stared at the tabletop, remembering childhood tales the adults had told her, some of which had kept her from sleeping. But what did she *really* know about strengi? She met Jenna's curious gaze. "I don't know."

Jenna reached across the table and put a hand on Alyse's wrist. "Do you trust me and Dorn?"

Alyse looked at Jenna. "Yes."

"Then you know Dorn and me would never do nothing to hurt you or Rill."

Anger sped through Alyse's body. She yanked her hand free. "Then why didn't you tell me about this strenga, Twalla, before?"

Dorn heaved another *humph*. "'Cause we thought you'd react like ya doin' now."

"And we thought Rill might get better," Jenna added gently.

"But he ain't," Dorn said. "So you gotta take him to Twalla."

Alyse's gaze jumped back and forth from Jenna to Dorn to Jenna while her mind struggled to absorb the stunning revelation.

"Strengi are healers," Jenna said. "And Twalla's one of the best. She cured Dorn of a serious illness—"

"I was *this* close to joinin' my ancestors." Dorn held up a thumb and forefinger, showing hardly any space between them.

Jenna nodded. "She's treated the rest of my family for ailments and injuries many times."

Her brow creased in deep furrows, Alyse mulled over what they had said. "If strengi are healers, why hasn't Priestess Sybil told me about them?"

"'Cause she's a mage," Jenna replied.

"But Priestess Sybil isn't that kind of woman. If she knew strengi can heal people, she'd accept them as fellow healers. I know she would."

Jenna responded with a shrug. "Maybe she ain't never met one. There ain't many strengi around nowadays. And the ones that are . . . well, they keep pretty much to themselves."

"They live in the countryside," Dorn said, "with poor folk like us."

"And we protect them," Jenna said. "We don't let outsiders know anything about 'em."

"I'm an outsider," Alyse said. "So why are you telling me?"

"'Cause Dorn and me trust you. And we thought Twalla might be able to help Rill."

Alyse shivered as an icy finger brushed down her spine. A strenga! *Goddess, help me!* Inhaling a deep breath, she straightened her shoulders and met Jenna's gaze full on. "I'll do whatever it takes to cure Rill."

Dorn slapped the tabletop. "'Atta girl!"

Jenna's lips curved into a warm smile. "Good. But you gotta promise to keep this a secret between you, me, Dorn, and Twalla."

Alyse responded instantly. "I promise."

Jenna fetched a basket made from narrow ribbons of split wood, with a carry handle, and stuffed it with bread, cheese, and vegetables. "For Twalla," she said in response to Alyse's questioning look. "To thank her for seein' us."

Jenna called Serin back in and told her she would be responsible for preparing supper. Then she and Alyse set out walking in the direction Alyse had been taking when she'd turned off the dirt road to Jenna's farm. The First Fruits' sun cast its fiery heat on them as they passed poor farms and an occasional noblesse villa. Gradually, their surroundings became more wooded, with narrow dirt paths leading to homes set so far off the road that they were hidden from view behind the trees. All the while, Alyse's apprehension mounted as she pictured herself confronting an ugly old hag in a hovel crammed with dead animals, poisonous plants, and deadly venoms to use in her potions.

At last, Jenna turned onto a barely discernible footpath that cut its way into a dense stand of trees. The nails of Alyse's clenched fingers bit into her palms while her heart drummed a rapid staccato beat. The trail ran straight for some distance, twisted, and ended at the edge of a large, grassy clearing with paving stones that led past a well to a small, tidy house made of clapboard walls and a thatched roof in the center. Smoke curled up into the blue, cloudless sky from the chimney. A small barn, with an enclosure in which two horses watched them with open curiosity, was on one side of the house. On the other side, a waist-high, rectangular stone wall surrounded a chicken coop where a rooster and chickens pecked the ground, and a milk cow chewed cud.

Jenna led Alyse along the cobbles to the house and knocked on the door. "Twalla, are ya home?"

A chunky girl around twelve years old opened the door. Her hair was the color of ripe wheat, and the brown dress she wore was clean. The girl's turquoise-colored eyes sparkled with pleasure when she saw Jenna. "Jenna," she said, a smile brightening her homely face. "Welcome to my mentor's house."

"Thank you, Laila," Jenna said, returning the smile. "Is your mentor at home?"

Laila stepped aside. "Come in and see for yourself."

In spite of Jenna's reassurances about Twalla, Alyse experienced a fluttering feeling in her belly while her instincts shouted at her to flee, and it took a lot of willpower for her to ignore them as she stepped over the threshold. Then she stopped involuntarily at the sight of a slender woman sitting at a trestle table well away from the hearth fire. The woman's back was to them, her long, dark-brown hair falling past her shoulders. Her right shoulder blade worked rhythmically, accompanied by the soft sound of something being ground.

Alyse shifted her eyes to Jenna, who motioned her to remain in place. Without saying a word, Jenna handed the basket to Laila, who took it into a back room. When Laila returned, she sat down at a table in a corner and began sorting through a large pile of herbs.

Alyse surveyed the room while her nerves wound tighter and tighter. The heat from the hearth fire made the place uncomfortably warm, but it also accented the pleasant fragrances from the herbs dangling from the rafters. A kettle hung from a crane in the hearth but was away from the cheerily crackling flames. Next to the hearth, a gray cat lay curled on a stool, sleeping. Shelves crammed with sealed earthenware jars lined the walls on two sides.

At last, Twalla's shoulder stopped moving, and she stood and turned to them.

Alyse's jaw dropped open in silent surprise when she found herself facing an attractive, brown-haired woman in her early thirties who looked at them through friendly blue eyes that matched the color of her dress.

"Jenna, how nice to see you," Twalla said, smiling. Her smile faded as her gaze slid to Alyse. "Who's your friend?"

"Her name's Alyse," Jenna said. "And I brought her here hopin' you could help her ailing friend."

The strenga smiled at Alyse. "I'm Twalla. Welcome to my home."

Twalla invited Alyse and Jenna to sit at the trestle table, then sat on the bench across from them. Jenna and Twalla made some small talk, mostly about Jenna's family and some neighbors, while Laila served them watered wine. All the while, Alyse reined in her impatience as she waited for Jenna to bring up the reason they'd come. She expelled a silent sigh when Twalla finally folded her hands on the tabletop and leaned toward her.

"Now, Alyse, tell me about your friend."

Alyse chewed on her lower lip, uncertain how to start. Just as she drew in a deep breath to begin telling her story, Jenna placed a hand on her wrist and spoke.

"First, Twalla, I hafta be honest with you. Alyse is noblesse."

A gasp of surprise shot out of Alyse's mouth, and she keyed herself for a strong reaction from the strenga. At the same time, a sense of betrayal from Jenna gushed through her in a roaring torrent, followed by disappointment. She had trusted Jenna. And now Twalla would refuse to treat Rill. But to Alyse's amazement, Twalla merely smiled.

"I could tell that as soon as I saw her." Twalla brushed a stray lock of dark-brown hair from her face. "But I don't think you would've brought her here, Jenna, if you didn't trust her."

Jenna nodded emphatically. "I do trust her. She's the healer who saved young Hilbrand Wistlow's life."

"Good Goddess!" Alyse said. "Does *everyone* around here know about that? It's supposed to be a secret."

"We country folk know how to keep our secrets," Twalla said. The cat, now wide awake, leaped off the stool onto the tabletop, and settled herself down in front of Twalla. Twalla stroked the cat, which set it to purring, while she looked directly into Alyse's eyes. "How did you end up here, and so far from Caldon?"

Alyse explained how she had run away from home to avoid a forced, loveless marriage to Troy Estati. How she had been captured by brigands and later rescued by a group led by Troy. And how Rill had been wounded by a Fire Bolt spell during a surprise attack by the vengeful brigands. "I couldn't go west to Caldon or east to The Marches," she concluded. "So I went south and ended up here."

Jenna patted Alyse's hand. "And the One Goddess brought her to our farm seeking refuge."

Twalla scratched her head while she shot Alyse a quizzical look. "You're a powerful healer in your own right. You cured Hilbrand's gangrene when he was near death. Why do you need my help?"

Twalla's question burst open the door holding back all Alyse's pent-up frustrations, anxieties, and fears. "Because I wasn't the one who cured him. It was a powerful healer who did that. I merely followed her instructions about how to mix the potion and cast the spell on it. If it hadn't been for her, Hilbrand would've died."

Twalla stroked the cat's neck with a thumb and forefinger, a thoughtful expression on her face. "So that's why you can't cure your friend."

"There's a malevolent energy in his wounds that I can't get rid of. And it's growing stronger every day. I think the treatment requires a potion and a spell." Alyse gulped down a ragged lungful of air. "But what they are, I don't know."

"And you thought I might," Twalla said.

Alyse nodded, her muscles tensing in expectation.

The cat rubbed her head against the strenga's chest, leaving gray fur on the blue dress. Twalla seemed not to notice. Alyse watched the healer, swallowing sobs that bubbled up into her throat. Finally, Twalla blinked and let out a long, deep sigh. "I'm a healer of everyday injuries and ailments, not wounds caused by magic."

Alyse choked on a huge sob. "So he'll die."

Leaning forward, Twalla grasped Alyse's hand. "No, no! Don't give up. There might still be a way."

Hope flared in Alyse's heart. "What is it?"

"You said a powerful healer cured Hilbrand?"

Alyse nodded eagerly. "Yes."

"But that *you* mixed the potion and cast the spell on it, not her."

"Yes."

"And that Hilbrand was near death."

"Yes. But . . . but what possible difference does that make? Hilbrand was consumed by gangrene. Rill is being consumed by Goddess knows what."

Twalla fingered the cat under its chin. "You healers apply your cures like you're following a recipe. For this ailment, apply that potion or cast that spell."

Alyse frowned. "Hmm . . . I never thought of it that way."

"We strengi work our healing differently."

"Why?"

"'Cause we don't know where our healing powers come from. All we know is that a few of us have that gift and that the powers reveal themselves to us in certain ways." Twalla nodded at Laila, who was working at the corner table. "We look for those signs when we choose apprentices who will carry on after we join our ancestors."

Alyse blew out an impatient sigh. "That's interesting. But what's it got to do with Rill's wound?"

Twalla held up a hand. "Patience." She resumed caressing the cat. "We strengi go back to Euloria and the Forbidden Lands long before the Great Destruction. We were healers, and refused to fight in the wars against Atland. We also wouldn't have nothin' to do with charms and staffs when the Eulorians began using 'em."

The cat stood, arched its back, crossed over to Alyse, and plopped down in front of her. Twalla smiled fondly at the cat, then looked up and met Alyse's gaze.

"We strengi believed that harnessing the energy of the magic plane was goin' against the ways of nature and of the One Goddess. So the charm wearers, who called themselves "mages," persecuted us. They labeled us 'strengi,' which means 'betrayers' in Eulorian. But it's them mages who were the true betrayers. Before charms and staffs, all knowledge of magic and access to magic came through this." Twalla tapped her head. "Through a sixth sense. We strengi still follow those ways. The Old Ways."

The Old Ways! A sudden spasm of dizziness struck Alyse, making it difficult to think. But the attack lasted only moments, and her light-headedness faded as she pondered what Twalla had said. The euloghi could access all forms of magic without using charms and staffs. They, and herself, were the descendants of the true mages, the ones who existed before charms and staffs were invented. Her brows plunged into a frown. Were Ulbra and Ulbridge Thane actually euloghi? Were their charms and staffs just props?

"Trial and error," Twalla was saying, apparently misreading Alyse's reaction to one of surprise at her revelation. "We've found that sometimes a potion that can cure one illness or help heal an injury also can do the same for other ones. What's important is the kinds of herbs in the potion and the power of your healing hands."

"We healers cast spells using our hands," Alyse said, her voice saturated with hope.

Twalla nodded. "Healing hands."

"So, are you suggesting I use the gangrene potion on Rill?" Alyse asked.

"If you can remember the ingredients and the amounts."

Alyse snorted. "I'll never forget them. But some aren't common. Do you think you'll have them all?"

Twalla chuckled, then pointed at the herbs hanging from the beams and at the jars lining the shelves, as the cat rose, turned around, and settled back down in front of Alyse. "I think I might." Then a hard look replaced the smile as she held Alyse's gaze. "Are you good at keeping secrets, Alyse Dejune?"

Alyse returned the look without blinking. "I'm *very* good at keeping secrets."

"That's good, because you must promise to tell no one about what you see, hear, or do here. Not even your friend Rill. This knowledge is a secret among the three of us."

"I promise."

Twalla slapped the tabletop, startling the cat, which leaped onto the floor and scampered off. "Then let's get started."

As Alyse named the ingredients one by one, Twalla pulled them from the hanging herbs or took them from the crocks. Then Twalla took the kettle off the crane, measured out the amounts, and dropped them into the kettle. Finally, she lifted the kettle back onto the crane and swung the crane over the crackling fire.

"Now," Twalla said as the flames began licking at the bottom of the kettle, "we stir and wait. And then you, Alyse, will cast our spell on its contents."

CHAPTER 13

Return

Alyse and Jenna arrived at the farm in the late afternoon. To Alyse, the return journey seemed to take twice as long as the trip to Twalla's because they had to lug the heavy iron kettle filled with the potion Twalla had mixed and cast the spell on. Alyse insisted on carrying the pot, but it was so heavy she could haul it only partway, holding the handle with both hands, before her arms gave out.

"Give it to me," Jenna said, and took the kettle from her.

Jenna carried the kettle the rest of the way, changing hands occasionally, but her pace never slackened.

As soon as Alyse entered the farmhouse, she hurried to Rill's room and bathed his side and thigh with the potion. She treated the wounds twice a day, morning and night. For the first three days, her inner eye detected no change in the malevolent energy. In fact, it seemed to be growing stronger instead of weaker. Discouragement washed over her like waves from an incoming tide. On the fourth day, when she still detected no change, doubts nibbled at her. Perhaps she'd missed one of the ingredients or had left out a word in the spell. Struggling to hold back her tears, she confided her fears to Jenna.

"Give it time," Jenna told her. "The magic might not start workin' right away."

"But it's been four days."

"And it's been more than that since Rill was wounded. Be positive. If you doubt yourself, it might affect your magic."

"Just like Palquo's evil might have affected his magic," Alyse said thoughtfully.

Jenna nodded. "Exactly."

On the fifth day, Alyse still detected no change. Now, despite her efforts to think positively, fear assaulted her mind, like legionaries attacking an enemy position. It took all her willpower to boot it out. She would *not* let Rill die. She placed her hands on Rill's side wound and applied healing hands for the longest time ever, all the while telling herself she didn't bring him all this way simply to have him die.

The next morning, she entered Rill's bedroom reluctantly, fearing she would find his condition even worse. Kneeling at Rill's bedside, she gently ran her hands along his body. Her hands stuck in place when she detected an imperceptible change in the malevolent energy. Then she sank onto the floor, her back against the bed, and burst into relieved laughter. The potion worked! She wanted to shout her joy loud enough for everyone on the farm to hear—Jenna and Serin in the kitchen, and Dorn and Tolle in the field—to inform them of her success. Instead, she let out a long, deep sigh, and her muscles relaxed as weariness crept into her bones.

By the end of the next week, Rill was sitting up in bed, his back propped against a straw-filled pillow. It didn't take him long before he became self-conscious about Alyse treating his side and thigh, and insisted on applying the potion himself.

Alyse rolled her eyes. "I'm a healer, Rill. I've seen a lot more of boys' and men's bodies than just their bare sides and thighs. Besides, it's not just the potion but also the power of my healing hands when I'm bathing your wounds with the potion that's destroying the malevolence inside you."

Rill gave in with a grumble, which made Alyse want to shake her head in amusement.

A week later, when Rill was well enough to get out of bed, Jenna gave him a shirt, vest, and pants that had belonged to her daughter's husband, Alard. "The clothes you wore were ruined," she told him. "So I cut 'em up for rags and altered these to fit you."

Rill seemed genuinely touched by the gift.

Even though Rill and Jenna appeared to get along well, Alyse detected a coldness between him and Dorn. Alyse mentioned their attitudes one day when she and Jenna were alone in the kitchen.

"Your friend Rill is a mage," Jenna responded. "Dorn ain't got no use for 'em. And now he has one living here under his roof. How would you feel in his place?"

"But I'm a mage too."

"Yeah. But you're a healer. You *help* people. You don't kill 'em or help your patrons to take their homes and livelihoods away."

Alyse had to admit she had a point.

Unlike Dorn, Tolle appeared to idolize Rill because he knew how to use a sword and a longbow, and because he had promised that when he was well enough to draw his bow, he would teach him how to shoot. But his grandson's friendliness toward Rill displeased Dorn. "I know how to use a sword too," he groused to Jenna and Alyse. "But you don't see Tolle fawnin' on me the way he does Rill."

Serin acted shyly around Rill but appeared to like him.

Eager to repay Jenna and Dorn for their kindness, Rill pestered Jenna to let him help with some of the lighter chores outside. "First Fruits season is almost here, and I'm sure he could use help with the crops." But she demurred and referred him to Dorn, who refused the offer. "Ya gotta recover your strength," Dorn told him, "not expend it. 'Cause the sooner you recover, the sooner you can leave. Besides that, ya don't know nothin' about farmin'."

Alyse and Jenna watched Rill stalk away from Dorn one day after Dorn had rejected yet another request to help him. Jenna turned to Alyse, a humorous glint in her hazel eyes. "Rill wants to help with the outdoor work, but I reckon helping with the *indoor* chores is beneath him."

The next day, around midmorning, Alyse was surprised to hear the rhythmic clanging of a hammer striking iron coming from behind the farmhouse. The sounds brought her and the entire Desfar family running to Alard's idle forge. The little smithy was no longer idle, and the charcoal in the forge was burning a bright yellow.

"Rill, your wounds!" Alyse cried. "You'll open them with all that movement."

Rill grinned at her, sweat rolling off his face. "I feel great! So everything will be fine." While he worked the bellows, he pointed with his chin at a hinge lying on the anvil. "It's a shame to let this old forge stand idle. So I thought I'd put it to good use by repairing the hinges on the barn door." His gaze homed in on Dorn. "I might not know farmin', but I *do* know blacksmithing."

"Let me see your side wound," Alyse said in a tone that brooked no dissent.

Grudgingly, Rill let her pull up his shirt to inspect the bandage.

A tight knot of anxiety formed in Alyse's chest. "Oh, Rill," she said, unable to hide her distress. "You've opened the wound, and the bandage is starting to absorb the blood." She grabbed the hammer from him, and turned to Dorn. "Put the forge fire out." She pivoted back to Rill. "You, come with me. You're going back to bed."

"But I ain't finished yet," Rill said, then grimaced from pain.

Alyse jabbed a finger in his chest. "Oh, yes you are."

Meekly, he followed her.

Rill spent the next several days in bed. Alyse only allowed him to get up again when he promised, by swearing an oath to the One Goddess, that he wouldn't do any physical activity, especially blacksmithing, until she gave him permission.

For Alyse, the time spent with the Desfar family had turned out to be the happiest period of her life. She had never before experienced being among a family whose members actually loved one another and worked in harmony to get things done. Sure, from time to time, they had disagreements and got angry with one another, but they always settled their differences amicably. That wasn't something her family did much. For the first time, Alyse also found herself letting her guard down. She didn't have to worry about deceptions, hidden meanings in words, concealed agendas, and being told she must do what's best to keep her family in power.

Alyse visited Twalla so often that they became friends. She even felt comfortable enough with Twalla to confess that she had pictured her as an ugly old hag. "You sure don't fit my image of a strenga!" Alyse ended with a laugh.

Twalla joined in her laughter, her blue eyes twinkling merrily. "And you're not what I pictured a mage healer to be, either."

Alyse and Twalla shared their knowledge about healing, traded recipes for potions and spells to cast on them, and exchanged anecdotes about interesting cases. They both ended up having increased respect for each other.

Alyse also took walks with Rill in the fields and woods near the Desfar farm. At first, she enjoyed spending time with him, but when they got talking, they always seemed to end up arguing. And the subject was usually about the noblesse. Their first disagreement occurred when they paused during their third walk to sit side by side on a small boulder to gaze at the woods and the surrounding land.

"I can hardly wait to get back to Caldon," Rill said as he snapped a twig in half and threw away one piece. "The Estati will have increased respect for me when I show up with you in tow. The Dejunes will too. With those two families supporting me, I'll have a better chance of becoming noblesse."

Alyse kept silent for a moment as his words sliced painfully into her heart. "I haven't said I'll go back with you," she told him in a quiet but firm voice.

Rill broke the remaining piece of twig in two. "You will."

Alyse clenched her jaw in annoyance. "You seem pretty sure of yourself."

"I am." Rill hurled one of the remaining pieces of twig after the first one. "Everyone else failed. Even Troy. But I succeeded. I brought you home to your family and your fiancée."

His smugness stoked Alyse's anger. She twisted around to face him. "Do you know what it's like being a noblesse?"

"Sure." Rill grinned. "You got power and magetas—you know, prestige. And everyone looks up to ya."

Alyse gave a mirthless laugh. "When you're outside looking in, you might think that. But when you're inside, you might see something quite different."

"Like what?" Rill asked, raising a skeptical eyebrow.

"Like having to do everything for your family."

"You mean, marrying Troy Estati?"

"That's right."

Rill ran his teeth along his lower lip. "Well, I'll admit that Troy ain't the nicest person in Caldon. But sometimes marrying someone you don't love is the price ya hafta pay to get what ya want."

Rill's offhand remark increased Alyse's anger, and it was all she could do not to slap him in the face. She took a deep breath to settle herself and said, "What do I want to 'get' by marrying Troy?"

Rill shrugged. "I guess you don't hafta want nothin'. You're noblesse. So you've already got it all. But me, I'm just a commoner, and I ain't got none of that. And I want it."

"Want what, exactly?"

A dreamy, faraway look appeared on Rill's face as if his mind had turned inward. He was silent for a moment, and then he spoke. "I wanna be elected to the Magesterium. And I wanna start my own noblesse-commoner family." He paused. "I wanna be someone important."

It took all Alyse's effort to swallow a biting retort. Rill was basically a good person, and she had to set him straight. "This is how you'll live your life as 'someone important.' You'll spend every day living inside a web of deception. Not being able to trust anyone, not even your parents and wife. Living in constant fear that you or your family might be assassinated or an enemy family might launch a charm raid on your compound. Marrying, or forcing your children to marry someone they don't love to further your family's interests. Are you willing to live like that? I'm certainly not."

Rill flung the last section of twig to the ground. "Well, I am!"

His sudden fury scared Alyse, but she remained in place and didn't let her fear show.

"Do ya know how old I was when I decided I wanted to become noblesse?" Rill asked.

Alyse shook her head.

"Nine. Jedd and I, we happened to be in the public square when a funeral procession came along. I don't even remember whose. But in my mind, I can still see them all walkin' down from The Citadel into the public square. Jedd and I climbed the Statue of the Twins to get a better look. What a sight!" He paused as if he were replaying the spectacle in his mind. "The funeral bier with the great man's corpse on it. The mourners walkin' in front of it, with the family members behind them. The actors wearin' the family's death masks following the bier. And all his clients walkin' behind them."

Rill's stubborn näiveté made Alyse want to get up and leave, but she resisted. "They're professional mourners," she said, struggling to keep sarcasm from her tone. "They were hired. So were the actors."

Rill dismissed her comment with a wave of his hand. "I know that. I ain't naïve. But so what? You don't see no commoners hiring 'em."

Alyse bit down on her tongue to prevent a snide remark from leaving her mouth.

"The crowd of people who came to watch," Rill said. "I'd never seen such a sight. And the speech that was given on the Speaker's Platform about the great man's deeds—"

"What deeds?"

Alyse's question made Rill fidget. "Well, I . . . umm . . . I don't remember them now. But they impressed me."

Alyse rolled her eyes toward the sky and invoked the One Goddess's help to keep her from snapping at Rill.

"Watching that funeral," he said, oblivious to Alyse's reaction. "That's when I vowed to become noblesse. Just like that man. And when I die, I'll have a funeral like his."

Despite her efforts, Alyse couldn't stop herself from laughing. "You want to become noblesse just so you can have a fancy funeral?"

A rush of red colored Rill's cheeks.

"I'd much rather be surrounded by the people I love," Alyse said. "And by those who love me."

"Stop baiting me!" Rill said, his voice sounding like a wolf's snarl. "That man had power, wealth, and respect."

"And maybe *you* should stop taking yourself so seriously."

Rill glowered at the Desfar farmhouse in the distance. He was silent for a long time, brooding. His attitude sent unease rippling up and down Alyse's spine. She touched his arm. "What are you thinking?"

"That I could of been noblesse. Did ya know that?"

Oh, Goddess, not this! Alyse didn't respond, hoping he would drop the subject. But he didn't.

"Did ya know that?" Rill asked, his tone insistent.

Alyse tossed a sideways glance at Rill. His jaw was tightly clenched, and his back was as straight as a mage's staff. She pictured anger smoldering in his blue eyes, ready to burst into flames. She chose to lie. "No, Rill. I didn't know that."

In a rush of raging words, Rill told her the story of how he learned that Livia Estati was his half sister, and Kendra Larkin had once been Deuth Estati's older sister, Carolyn. "I could of been an Estati," he ended. "I could of been noblesse."

"Oh, Rill." Alyse put a hand on his arm. "If your mother had stayed married to Brico Svagga, you would never have been born. Or, if she'd had a son, that boy wouldn't be you because your father would've been Brico, not Marc."

Rill jumped to his feet and towered over her, his eyes flashing anger like blue lightning bolts. "If my mom hadn't married my dad, the Estati would've accepted me as one of their family. I would of been noblesse. Lord Deuth told me so himself. But she did marry him. A . . . a *blacksmith*." Determination burned on Rill's face like a raging fire. "Lord Deuth took me on as his apprentice. He's givin' me a chance to become noblesse. And, by Goddess, I'm takin' that chance. I'm gonna be a mage, and I'm gonna be noblesse. And no one and no thing's gonna stop me."

After a few more conversations like that, Alyse stopped her walks with Rill and spent more time with Twalla instead. Rill seemed puzzled about why she was always too busy whenever he suggested a stroll, and apparently it never occurred to him that he was the reason. His lack of self-awareness saddened Alyse, but if she brought it up, she knew it would just lead to another argument.

One afternoon during dinner, Rill announced to Alyse that he was fit enough to travel and that they would leave for Caldon in the morning. Angered by his insensitivity, she argued with him in front of the Desfars, who were sitting across the table from them.

"So you made up your mind that we should leave tomorrow without even consulting me," she said, her hands shaking so much from anger that she hid them on her lap.

Rill shrugged. "What's there to consult about?"

"That perhaps I don't want to go?"

Rill flicked her words away with a casual wave of his hand. "I serve the Estati, not you. And my job is to take you back so ya can marry Lord Troy."

"And if I don't want to go?" Alyse asked, her green eyes burning into his. "Then I'll—"

"She ain't goin' back," Dorn said firmly.

Rill's eyes pierced his like two arrows shot from a longbow. "What did ya say?"

Dorn half rose and leaned toward Rill until their faces were only two hand widths apart. "I said, if Alyse don't wanna go back, she ain't goin' back."

Rill fired him a scornful look. "And who's gonna stop me—you?"

"If I hafta."

Rill laughed.

Dorn rose to his full height, anger infusing every wrinkled line in his face.

Alyse jumped to her feet and stretched out her arm, palm out. "No, wait! I'm going back with him."

Dorn froze and swung his gaze to Alyse. "Ya don't hafta if ya don't wanta."

"But I *do* want to," Alyse said. "I told you about my cousin, Kate. Troy and the others took her back to Caldon as a prisoner. If they managed to avoid the brigands, they're all back there now. Kate's not just my backwatcher and cousin. She's my best friend too. I know my matriarch punished her for helping me run away and for coming with me as well. I have to do whatever I can to help her. And if that means returning to Caldon as Rill's 'prisoner,' then so be it."

Dorn lobed a withering look at Rill as if it were a stone flung by a slinger. "Lucky for you."

The next morning, Alyse and Rill departed on the now-recovered mare. Alyse sat behind Rill with her arms wrapped around his waist as they headed up the dusty road. Alyse could feel the Desfars' eyes on them until she and Rill disappeared from sight. She wished she could repay them for their kindness in taking her and Rill in. And thank Twalla as well. If it weren't for her, Rill would be dead.

Then a powerful wave of foreboding washed away those thoughts. Alyse resisted the sudden urge to slip off the mare and race back to the safety of the Desfars. She was going home. Back into the hot, bubbling cauldron of expectations she had fled. But she had no choice because Troy had taken

Kate back as a prisoner, and Ariella Estati was bound to expel Kate because she had helped Alyse flee an unwanted marriage to Troy.

Would she find Kate, or would her cousin be lost to her forever? Perhaps Kate had gone to live in The Slums as a dagger woman or run off to join a band of brigands. Alyse really couldn't picture Kate doing either, but what other alternatives did her cousin have? Then Alyse's thoughts turned to herself, making her body tremble and her heartbeat sluggish. Her family would be furious with her for running away, and Grandmother Maude might expel her. She would become homeless, an outcast rejected by all the First and Lesser Families.

What sort of future did she face?

Turn the Page to See
A Sneak Peek of the
Current Draft of
Book 3

Revenge of the Estatis

CHAPTER 1

Charm and Staff

RILL RESISTED THE URGE urge to let his shoulders sag in relief as they passed through the Public Gate into Caldon. He uttered a silent prayer thanking the One Goddess that the uncomfortable part of the journey was almost finished. A dog's sudden bark interrupted his thoughts, and a hound dashed toward him. Alyse tightened her grip around Rill's waist as the mare shied away from the dog.

"Are you alright?" Rill asked after the dog ran past them.

Alyse didn't respond.

Rill shrugged off her silence. After all those days in the saddle with her, he was used to it.

He bypassed the Public Square and started up the gray cobblestone road leading to the top of The Citadel. Reaching the crest, Rill turned the mare's head left instead of right.

Alyse yanked in on Rill's belly, making him expel a lungful of air. "Hey, wait! Where are you going? That's not the way to my home."

Rill ground his teeth in annoyance. Alyse had been a pain in the butt all the way home, day after day reminding him that she was *allowing* him bring her back to Caldon only because she was concerned about her cousin, Kate Dejune, Knowing Alyse's family, Rill figured her matriarch had already expelled Kate because she had helped Alyse in her aborted attempt to avoid marrying Troy Estati. He figured Alyse knew that, too, but refused to admit it to herself. "We ain't goin' there."

Rill felt her body stiffen. "You're taking me to the Estatis?"

Rill performed a mental eyeroll. *What does she expect—that everyone will welcome her back with open arms?* "They're the ones who sent me after you. So they're the ones I'm deliverin' you to."

Pride swelled Rill's chest. All during the trip back, he'd imagined the brouhaha everyone would make when he showed up at the Estati compound. He had accomplished what no one else, not even Troy, could do.

As soon as he drew rein in the courtyard, off-duty protectors and back-watchers, chattering with excitement, surrounded him. Their babbling stopped abruptly when the front door burst open and Deuth, Troy, and the Estati women stepped into the bright afternoon sunshine. They stopped short when they spotted him sitting tall in the saddle. Rill savored the stunned expression on their faces, as if he were tasting a fine, vintage wine.

Deuth walked through a space the onlookers silently opened for him. The rest of the Estatis trailed behind him.

"Rill," Deuth said as he stopped by the mare, "we thought you both were dead." He patted Rill's leg. "Well done, Rill. Well done."

Anger swirled in Alyse's face and her emerald-green eyes turned hard, but she said nothing.

Rill's lungs expanded with pleasure, and he sat even taller, feeling like a conqueror. "Obviously, we ain't dead." He forced his expression to become solemn, then nodded at the Estatis' matriarch who had stopped beside Deuth. "Lady Ariella, I've fulfilled the charge you gave me. I've brought back Lady Alyse Dejune."

Ariella's blue eyes sparkled with approval. "You've more than fulfilled my expectations, Rill." The sparks turned white-hot, her lips tightened into a parchment-thin line, and her brows plunged into a deep frown as she turned her gaze to Alyse. "Get off that horse, you little piece of baggage."

Alyse slipped down in an easy, fluid motion. Then, spine straight and shoulders erect, she steadily shoved back the stony gaze Ariella pressed against her. Neither spoke.

The onlookers glanced from one to the other as the tension rose like a lute string being tightened until it snapped.

"Alyse Dejune," Ariella finally said, "you've insulted my son, my family, my ancestors, and our future generations by your actions. I have a good mind to cancel our alliance with your family."

Alyse pulled herself erect, somehow managing to look dignified despite her travel-worn clothes, dirty face, and disheveled chestnut hair. "I did what I thought was best. Now you must do the same."

Ariella took a quick step toward her and slapped her face. The sharp impact sounded like a crack of thunder.

"You just overstepped yourself, Lady Ariella," Alyse said, her green eyes hard as uncut emeralds, as she put a hand to the red bruise forming on her cheek."

Anger burned brightly in Ariella's dark blue eyes while she glared at Alyse. "And so have you. You're not my matriarch. You have no authority over me."

"Soon you'll be Troy's wife, and I'll be your mother-in-law." Ariella yanked Alyse's arm. "Between your matriarch and me, we'll teach you to obey."

Alyse jerked free. "That remains to be seen."

Ariella nodded at Troy. "Take her home. And *this* time, try not to lose her."

Troy started toward Alyse.

"No! I'll not go home with a coward. Someone who abandoned Rill to the brigands so he could save his own skin. I refuse to marry a coward."

Troy froze mid-step, as if she'd cast a Paralyze spell on him.

Bewilderment formed on Ariella's face. Deuth appeared just as puzzled. Confusion rippled through the retainers, but Troy remained unnaturally still while a blush bloomed on his face.

Ariella turned to Troy. "That's not what you told us. You said the brigands killed Alyse and Rill in the attack at the crossroads."

Troy opened his mouth a couple of times, as if he were trying to force words out but couldn't. "Well . . . umm . . ." Then the words zipped out, each chasing the heels of the other. "I *thought* they'd been killed. Brigands had surrounding them and mages were casting Fire Bolt spells at them."

"Lies!" Alyse bent toward Troy, her eyes scrunched into angry slits. "I guess you didn't tell anyone that I was sitting behind you on your horse. When I told you we had to go back to help Rill, you refused. I saving your own skin was more important than helping your uncle's loyal apprentice who was facing the brigands alone."

Deuth stepped toward Troy, brows narrowed. "Is that true?"

Troy turned a panicky face to Deuth, then focused on Ariella. "She's lying! Don't listen to her."

"Let her have her say," Ariella commanded.

Alyse shot Troy a look of utter disgust, then turned to Ariella. "There were only four brigands. All mages, including Palquo, the brigands' leader. They cast two Fire Bolt spells on Rill." She stroked the mare. "And a third on this poor horse." She strode up to Troy and faced him, nose-to-nose. "You left Rill to die while you galloped off to safety. And you left me there as well. You're a coward with a yellow streak down your back wider this this entire compound."

Alyse turned to Rill. "Tell them that's so."

Dread suddenly overwhelmed Rill and he took a series of quick, shallow breaths. Alyse had backed him into a corner. By supporting her against Troy, he might lose the Estatis' support. He swallowed a mouthful of saliva that, like a slimy snake, had crept up his throat into his mouth. "Well, I . . ." He cleared his throat. "I remember bein' struck by Palquo's fire bolts. Then everything went blank. When I woke up, I was being dragged on a litter by this here horse, and you was walkin' beside me."

The look, brimming with contempt, that Alyse leveled at him made Rill want to pull his head deep down inside his shirt.

Alyse turned to Ariella. "I don't need an escort. I'll go by myself."

"You'll not go without an escort," Ariella said. "The Estatis brought you back and the Estatis will deliver you to your matriarch."

"I'll escort her," Livia said.

Before Ariella could reply, Livia rushed over to Alyse and together they strode through the gate, Alyse leading her horse by its reins. Rill's gaze lingered on Alyse as she mounted the mare and started off along the cobbles with Livia walking beside her. She held her shoulders back and her head high, a portrait of pride. Two conflicting emotions wrestled for domination in Rill— shame for not supporting her and relief that she was gone. A thought settled uneasily on his shoulders. Was he a coward for not supporting her in her accusations against Troy? He gave an imperceptible shake of his head. Naw.

He fought the brigands at their camp and at the crossroads. So he wasn't no coward. He just wanted to make something of himself, come Shelar or high water.

Ariella's voice pierced his thoughts. "What are you standing around for?" she said to the crowd of protectors and backwatchers. "You all have things to do. So do them."

Then she strode into the house.

The rest of the family followed her, except for Deuth. He draped an arm around Rill's shoulder. "I'm afraid you've made an enemy of my nephew."

"He's been an enemy for quite some time," Rill wanted to say, but he shrugged instead.

"Let's go into my study," Deuth said.

After closing the door, Deuth waved Rill into a chair and then sat down at his desk.

As Rill settled into the chair, his nerves tied themselves into painful knots. Was Lord Deuth going to stop mentoring him because he'd humiliated Troy not just in front of the Estati family but in front of their retainers too?

Deuth picked up a white quill pen, leaned back in the chair, and fiddled with the quill, a frown on his face, as if he were gathering his thoughts. Finally, he sat straight and said, "Don't expect any thanks from Lady Ariella for bringing Alyse back. Alyse's running away humiliated her and the rest of our family. Even worse, having you bring her back instead of Troy has shamed her even more." He waved the feathered end at Rill and grinned. "But, speaking for myself, I'm proud of you."

Deuth's praise made Rill's skin tingle all over, and he strove to keep a grin from conquering his face. "Thank you, Lord."

Deuth ran a finger along the quill's shaft. "I'd like to reward you, but I can't do that openly. Perhaps sometime in the future, when tempers simmer down, I can."

Rill hesitated, wondering if he should bring up the matter. But now, because he was in Deuth's good graces, was probably the best time. "Maybe there is something you can do now, Lord."

Deuth tossed the quill onto the desktop. "What's that?"

His heart tapping a tattoo against his ribs, Rill took a deep breath and leaned forward in the chair. "I think I've been an able apprentice."

"That you have."

"I've shown you I can use a Warrior charm. I've collected debts for you faithfully. And now I brought Lady Alyse back when Lord Troy couldn't—"

Deuth held up a hand. "Let's not go there. But, yes. That's all true. So what's your point?"

Rill hesitated while he gathered his courage before answering while the tattoo against his chest increased. He ran a nervous tongue across his lips. "Give me my own charm and staff. I believe I've earned them."

A pained expression scuttled across Deuth's face. "I'm afraid that's not possible."

Deuth's response created a sudden coldness in Rill's chest. "Why not?"

"Because things aren't that simple."

"What do ya mean?"

"Where's your staff?"

"I ain't got it."

Deuth raised strict eyebrows.

A flush of embarrassment heated Rill's cheeks. "I lost it in the fight at the crossroads."

"That's most unfortunate because staffs are in short supply." Deuth drummed his fingers on the desktop for a long moment, a frown on his face, as if he were thinking. "And your charm? You still have that, I assume, although I don't see a chain around your neck. Or did something happen to the charm?"

An invisible hand grabbed Rill's heart and the tattoo ceased in mid-beat. "I lost it too. In the fight at the crossroads."

Deuth half rose from the chair. "How in the name of the One Goddess could you lose your charm? It was around your neck."

"I don't know, Lord," Rill said, rushing his words together. "One of the brigands must of taken it when I was unconscious."

Deuth's eyes opened so wide the whites showed. "Do you know the value of a staff and a charm?"

Rill looked down, his heart slowing to sluggish thumps. "Priceless."

"They're more than priceless," Deuth said, his voice so cold it made Rill shiver. "Irreplaceable. Both of them."

"I'm sorry, Lord."

Deuth made a derisive snort. "'Sorry.'" He snorted again. "How will being *sorry* bring back my family's charm and staff?"

Rill couldn't think of a suitable reply, so he said nothing.

"Well?" Deuth asked, his tone harsh, after a long, uncomfortable silence.

"It won't," Rill said in a tiny voice, his gaze still focused on the mosaic floor while the extra-slow thumping of his heart pounded in his ears.

"Exactly. Which brings us back to why it's impossible for me to *lend* you another charm and staff." He paused for what seemed to Rill and excruciatingly long moment. "Because that charm and staff were going to be yours after you proved yourself by bring back Lady Alyse."

"Mine?" Astonishment made Rill's heartbeats quicken. Then he frowned, puzzled. "But you told me I'd hafta steal a charm and staff to prove myself."

"True," Deuth said, giving a quick nod. "But I changed my mind. After all, you were almost family. So Lady Ariella had decided to let you keep the charm and staff you already had." His eyes narrowed. "The ones you lost."

"But you've got extra charms and staffs in your charm vault. I saw them when you took me there to show me the *Book of Charms*."

"By losing the ones we lent you, you showed us you can't be trusted with another set. At least, not another set of ours."

A sense of hopelessness settled on Rill's shoulders, feeling so heavy he slumped in his chair. "What am I gonna do?"

"You can ask your mother that," Deuth said. "She's the one who's responsible for the mess you're in."

Anger bubbled inside Rill like molten lava in a volcano ready to erupt sky high. His mom! "I could of been an Estati if it wasn't for her. If she hadn't renounced your family—*her* family—and married my dad."

Deuth nodded, his face a mask of righteous anger. "We would've accepted you as an Estati faster than an eye blink. You would've been entitled to your own charm and staff as a birthright. Just like Troy and Livia were given theirs."

Deuth got up from behind the desk and put a hand on Rill's shoulder. "Your own mother denied you your birthright." He whispered the next words in Rill's ear. "She hates you."

The words made Rill flinch. "She don't hate me." But even as he spoke, his stomach quivered ever so slightly, and doubt snuck into his mind, like an enemy legionary creeping up on a sentry.

"She does," Deuth said. "That's why she denied you your birthright to be an Estati. To have your own charm and staff—not on loan, but as your own Goddess-given right."

The volcano brewing inside Rill finally erupted. "I hate her!"

"As she does you," Deuth said. "But we don't hate you. Just the opposite. We see you as *almost* a member of the family. *Almost* an Estati." Deuth put his other hand on Rill's other shoulder and gazed at him with eyes bursting with compassion. "I want you to become one of us, Rill. An Estati. So I'll tell you what I'm going to do." Deuth paused, as if he had trouble believing what he was about to say next. "I'll defy my matriarch."

Rill lurched in the chair, stunned by Deuth's words.

"I know where you can get a charm and staff. And I'll even help you get them so you can claim your them as your birthright."

A lump of gratitude for this wonderful man formed in Rill's throat that was so massive he could hardly choke his words out. "How can I ever repay you?"

Deuth smiled down at him, his features bursting with magnanimity. "Oh, I'm sure we'll find a way."

CHAPTER 2

Homecoming

APPREHENSION CURLED IN ALYSE'S belly like a deadly, poisonous snake, fed by the rhythmic clopping of her mare's hooves on the cobblestones leading to the family compound. She and Livia paused at the front gate.

Amazement showed on the faces of the protectors who stood guard outside. One of them slid back the wooden covering of a small window in the gate and whispered, "It's Lady Alyse! She's not dead. She's here. Inform Lady Maude."

Moments later, Alyse heard startled voices crying her name and then the sound of boots slapping against cobbles as someone raced off inform the family of her return. The *slap slap* of her own heart against her chest matched the slaps of the boots. She braced herself, straightening her body in the saddle, and had the mare walk through the now-open gate. Livia strode alongside her, and Alyse found the warmth of Livia's presence comforting.

Off-duty protectors and backwatchers crowded around Alyse, Livia, and the horse, their voices babbling joyful welcomes. The expressions on their faces showed a collage of shock, surprise, incredulousness, and delight.

Jade elbowed her way through the press of bodies dressed in tan, red-striped livery and stopped by the mare as Alyse was dismounting. She grabbed Alyse's arm. "You're coming with me."

Alyse yanked her arm free. "You don't give me orders. I give *you* orders."

"I was sent to bring you back—"

"And you failed. Now I've returned on my own accord."

Jade glowered at her, nostrils flaring.

"That's right," Livia said. "Lady Alyse—"

Jade spun to face her. "Butt out! This is Dejune business, not Estati."

Livia bared her teeth and was about to spit out a retort when the front door banged open and Lady Maude strode out, followed by Maude, Pilar, Mora, Jukka Berne, and Degas Spicer. The retainers broke ranks to let them through.

Pilar wrapped her arms around Alyse and drew her in close. "My child, we thought you were dead," she said in a shaky voice. "That brigands killed you. Thank the One Goddess you're not."

Alyse smiled warmly, delighted by Pilar's motherly affection. "As you can see, I'm very much alive."

Maude hugged Alyse, too, then drew back and scanned her up and down with her flint-gray eyes. Warmth infused her voice. "I'm happy to see that you're alive." She smiled and patted Alyse cheek. "Now Mora doesn't have to marry Troy."

Alyse stepped back, colliding against the stirrup iron hanging down the mare's flanks. A sharp streak of pain shot up and down her back. "I didn't come home to marry Troy. I came home to find Kate."

Maude's jaws tightened so hard her cheeks bulged. "You won't find her here."

The words struck Alyse in the chest like dagger thrusts. She had thought this might happen and had prepared herself for it, but not enough because her guts were lurching in her belly, like a ship being pounded in a stormy sea. "Where is she?"

"I could care less."

"I'll find her."

"You'll do no such thing." Maude turned to Jade. "Lock Lady Alyse in her bedroom and give the key to me."

Jade grabbed hold of Alyse's arm and hauled her off like a common criminal. When they reached Alyse's bedroom, Jade shoved her past the threshold, then closed and locked the door.

Alyse opened the shutters on the window, then paced back and forth across the multi-colored tiles on mosaic floor, unable to focus on her own predicament because of her worry about Kate's. What had Maude done to her? The question ate at her, making her picture the worst scenarios. Kate had spent most of her life living here. She had no close friends besides the ones she had made here, and now everyone had been forced to turn against her. Had Kate fled to The Slums? There wasn't much use for an honest woman there. It seemed to Alyse that Kate's only options were to become a dagger woman or a prostitute, but Alyse couldn't picture her as either. Or perhaps she'd left Caldon entirely. But where would she go and how could she earn a living. Joining a band of brigands was the only likely option, but if she encountered Palquo's band, they would kill her.

Alyse flinched in surprise when the door connecting her bedroom to Kate's opened and Mora walked in.

A nasty smile contorted Mora's face. "Happy to see me?" Mora held up a key. "Grandmother Maude forgot about the lock for this door. I'll be sure to remind her."

"What do you want?"

Mora leaned her back against the door. "You were curious about Kate. So I thought I'd relieve your mind."

Mora had come to taunt her, but Alyse would play the game if Mora would end up giving her the answer. "Where is she?"

"Gone.

"Gone where?"

Grandmother Maude expelled her. Stripped her of all her clothes except for her shift and sent her on her way." Mora's lips twisted into a sneer. "It was quite a sight. The talk of The Citadel." She snickered. "Some of the kids even threw stones at her. I saw one hit her head and another her shoulder."

Mora's vindictiveness snapped Alyse's feigned calmness. She lunged at Mora, but Mora sidestepped and punched her in the stomach. Alyse doubled over as her breath whooshed out of her mouth.

"Don't you *ever* touch me again," Mora said.

Alyse straightened, her hands clutching her belly. "Where is she?"

Mora sniggered. "I'll tell you the honest truth: I don't know."

"Don't lie to me!"

"I'm not. The fact is, no one knows. And no one cares." She turned and started through the adjoining door to Mora's room. Then she stopped, turned, and held up the key. "Oh, I'll lock the door and give the key to Grandmother."

Sometime later, a handywoman changed the locks on both doors. A short time after that, a pair of handywomen closed and nailed the shutters on Alyse's windows from the outside, plunging the bedroom into darkness. Fortunately, the twin oil lamps on Alyse's dressing table and the one on the nightstand still contained oil, and she lit all three. No one had taken the logs by the fireplace, but it wasn't cold enough to for a fire.

Alyse found a book, laid down on the bed, and began reading. Just as she had lost herself in the book, she heard a key rattling in the door's lock. Alyse scrambled to her feet just as the door opened.

Jade walked in and shoved a thin sheath of note parchment at her.

"What's this for?" Alyse asked.

Jade crossed to the dresser and inspected the small ink pot. Apparently satisfied, she set the pot down.

Confusion swirled in Alyse's mind at Jade's weird actions. "Jade, what's going on?"

Jade pointed at the parchment.

Alyse unfolded the small piece of vellum and read Grandmother Maud's words in the shimmering yellow light of the two lamps on the dresser. *You will remain locked in your room, in darkness and silence, until you agree to marry Troy. Until then, you will only eat bread and water.*

Alyse glanced at Jade who mimed writing on her hand with an invisible quill pen, then crossed her arms and waited. Her message was obvious. Alyse's first instinct was to crumple and fling the parchment at Jade, but she forced herself to take a few deep breaths to calm herself in this new game of competing wills her grandmother had chosen to play with her.

Alyse was tempted to write, "Let the game begin." Instead, she scribbled, "I will *not* marry Troy!"

The game of will-against-will had now begun.

###

A key scraped in the lock, the door opened, and Jade entered the darkened bedroom carrying Alyse's . . . what? Breakfast? Lunch? Supper? Being cooped up in the dark with the shutters nailed shut and the only light provided by a single, tiny oil lamp on the dressing table had jumbled Alyse's sense of time. She had already given up trying to figure out how many days had passed since she'd been locked up. She also had stopped trying to talk with Jade, who had become her jailer, because Jade ignored every communication attempt. Alyse heaved a weary shrug that was invisible in the gloom. Grandmother Maude had told her she would live in darkness and silence until she agreed to marry Troy. So be it.

Alyse welcomed the torchlight shining in from the family area when Jade opened the door and also seeing a servant walking by. Jade pushed the door closed with the heel of her boot while she held the food tray in both hands. Alyse waited silently, her stomach growling for sustenance. She had stopped trying to engage Jade in conversation—even just a few words—because Jade ignored each attempt. Jade was only following orders, of course, but Alyse assumed Jade relished her control over her.

Jade set the plain earthenware plate and mug on the dressing table, near the lamp, and turned toward Alyse.

Alyse clenched her hands, her fingernails biting into her palms, because she knew what was coming next in this deadly charade.

Jade mimed writing on her hand with an invisible quill pen, then crossed her arms and waited. The invisible message was, as always, the same.

Her mind burning with anger, Alyse grabbed a real quill from the dressing table, dipped it in the ink bottle, and scribbled a reply on the stop sheet of a stack of parchments she'd been given: "I will *not* marry Troy!" Then she sanded and folded the note and thrust it at Jade.

After Jade left, Alyse went to the table and stared at the tray. She wrinkled her nose at what the dancing, yellow flame revealed: another hunk of crusty bread and a mug of wine that had been watered down until it almost tasted like water. Alyse had always enjoyed the smell of bread baking in the ovens by the hearth in the kitchen. And she loved its smell of the bread when the cooks took the crusty loaves out of the oven. Most of all, her mouth watered at the prospect of the head cook's giving her a warm, thick slice of bread to munch on. But not anymore. After having to eat slabs of stale, days-old bread for every meal, she now despised the stuff. She wondered if, once she was released from her perpetually dark prison, she would regain her taste for bread. She hoped so.

She ate a tentative bite of bread. She had learned the hard way, because the bread's interior could be just as hard as its crust, as if it had been left to dry out long enough to cut her mouth. And Alyse believed that sometimes the kitchen staff had been ordered to do just that—to let the bread turn hard—to make her incarceration more painful. Fortunately, this piece wasn't so bad. Probably just a couple of days old. Thankfully, she wouldn't have to soak each fragment she broke off in the precious, so-called watered wine to soften it.

Alyse broke off another chunk. She ate all the bread, no matter how stale, because she had to keep up her strength. Her stomach rumbled from hunger as she sipped some more watered wine. She had to ration the wine until the next time Jade came in with her food because it was the only liquid she was given, one mug per meal.

Alyse swallowed a lump of bread. *Grandmother Maude won't break me.* How many times had she vowed that to herself? At least fifty since . . . when? Yesterday? Two days ago? Four days ago? Yet she had no idea how many meals she had gotten.

"A few times," Jade told her once, in that scornfully jeering manner Alyse had come to hate, "you've gotten just two meals a day. And occasionally just one."

Alyse wondered if Jade had spoken the truth or was just toying with her. To add to Alyse's confusion about the passage of time, Jade periodically replaced the oil lamp with different-sized ones. That mean trick, which Grandmother Maude had probably ordered, made it impossible for Alyse to estimate the passage of time by how long it took the lamp to run out of oil.

The bread eaten and the wine mug half emptied, Alyse laid down on her bed, closed her eyes . . .

And was startled to wakefulness by the sound of a key grating in the lock of the door. Alyse squinted, almost blinded by the torchlight flaming in the family area beyond the door, as Jade entered. Alyse pushed herself into a sitting position, her feet on the floor.

Jade handed Alyse another note, which was from Grandmother Maude: "Your next food allotment will be cut in half unless you agree to marry Troy."

Alyse made a scoffing noise in her throat. "Getting impatient is she?"

Jade held out her hand and twitched her fingers, indicating she expected a response.

Alyse pushed herself onto her feet, went to the dressing table, and scribbled one word on parchment: "No!" She folded the parchment in two, then thrust it at Jade. "Tell my grandmother to chew on this."

Jade took the paper and left.

Alyse sank back onto the bed. Grandmother Maude wouldn't break her.

Time dawdled. Meals arrived with increasingly smaller portions of bread and watered wine that finally became all water and the cup containing it became smaller too. Gradually, Alyse became indifferent to her stomach's constant grumbling until the rumbling gradually disappeared. She turned lethargic and began spending all her time lying in bed, staring into blankness. Memories of her favorite foods plodded through her mind, but her mouth was too dry to salivate. She vaguely thought that she had missed her sacred time of the month but didn't really care if she had. After a while, it became an effort to get up and go to the bathroom in the bucket they'd given her, which wasn't a big deal because nothing much ever came out anymore. . . .

Alyse didn't hear the key grate in the lock as Jade opened the door and placed a thin sliver of bread and a tiny cup of water on the nightstand. Alyse motioned for her to leave with a listless wave of her hand. And she hardly noticed Jade pick up the oil lamp from the dressing table, hold the lamp over her face while she eyed her, and then silently leave. All Alyse wanted to do was sleep. . . .

A hand on her shoulder stirred Alyse into semi-consciousness. She blinked, blinded by the harsh glare of a lantern held by her head, and saw a blurry face hovering over her. She struggled to put an arm over her eyes to protect them from the lantern's glare.

"Alyse," a familiar voice said softly.

Alyse fished around in her groggy brain to identify it but couldn't.

"Alyse," the voice repeated.

"Huh?"

"Don't you think it's time?"

"Huh?"

A gentle hand touched her shoulder. "It's time to stop this foolishness."

"Time?"

"Yes. Time to marry Troy."

Alyse removed her arm from over her eyes with the slowness of a caterpillar. She blinked rapidly as the glaring light revealed the hazy facial features merged into a sharper image . . . her mother's face.

"Don't . . . wanna . . . marry . . ."

"Nonsense," Pilar said softly. "Troy loves you. That hardly ever happens in a noblesse marriage. You're a very lucky girl."

"Don't . . . wanna . . ."

"Come on, now." Pilar eased Alyse into a sitting position and adjusted the pillow. "I have some tasty broth for you." She motioned to a servant Alyse hadn't noticed standing behind her mother, holding a soup bowl and a spoon. Pilar brushed her fingers lightly along Alyse's cheek. "We don't want you to die."

Alyse barely heard Pilar's words because she was eying the soup bowl.

"You have your whole life ahead of you to live." Pilar motioned for the servant, who handed her the bowl and spoon. "Now, dear, swallow this."

Alyse didn't have the energy to resist, so she went along and swallowed the warm broth that Pilar gently spooned into her mouth.

"Your grandmother was against me doing this," Pilar said as Alyse swallowed more of the tasty broth. "But I don't want you to starve to death because of your bullheadedness." Pilar nodded for the servant to wipe soup dribble from Alyse's chin. "But she finally relented, for just this once. She'll give you another chance. So think carefully about it because it's your last chance."

Alyse barely heard her mother's words as she swallowed spoonful after spoonful of the delicious broth until Pilar returned the now-empty bowl to the servant.

Pilar put a gentle hand on her shoulder. "Tell me you'll marry Troy."

Alyse lay back onto the bed, her body and mind too weak to resist, and mumbled a response. "All right." Then, through dimly focused eyes, she saw her mother smile

"That's my girl. I'll send Lenia the healer here to check on you."

As the door clicked shut behind her mother and the servant, Alyse rested her arm on her forehead. The vague notion that she had lost her fight drifted slowly through her mind, like a feather on a gentle current of air.

But she didn't care.

17

Dan Lutts was born and lived in Quincy, Massachusetts before bouncing around the country and ending up in Maine. He grew up reading science fiction, then turned to historical fiction, history and, more recently, Young Adult fiction.

Lutts spent most of his career first as a history teacher and then as a writer and editor in high tech and other fields. When he's not working or writing, Dan can be found reading or playing with his two dogs and two cats—all rescue animals.

We've come to the end of this part of Rill and Alyse's story. I love to paint verbal pictures that draw readers into a fictional world and the characters who live there. Stories that leave you wanting to know what happens to them next. I hope I've succeeded. But whether I have or not is up to you, the reader.

Now I'm supposed to give you a link to Amazon or goodreads or some other website to make it easier for you to leave a review. But I'm not doing that. You know how to leave a review if you enjoyed the book. As always, the choice is yours.

www.ingramcontent.com/pod-product-compliance
Lightning Source LLC
Chambersburg PA
CBHW051229210726
48290CB00003B/863